PAMELA

PAMELA

Mary Mackie

Chivers Press · Thorndike Press
Bath, England   Thorndike, Maine USA

This Large Print edition is published by Chivers Press, England, and by Thorndike Press, USA.

Published in 2000 in the U.K. by arrangement with HarperCollins Publishers Ltd.

Published in 2000 in the U.S. by arrangement with Juliet Burton Literary Agency.

U.K. Hardcover ISBN 0–7540–3989–7 (Chivers Large Print)
U.K. Softcover   ISBN 0–7540–3990–0 (Camden Large Print)
U.S. Softcover   ISBN 0–7862–2308–1 (General Series Edition)

The text of this Large Print edition is unabridged.
Other aspects of the book may vary from the original edition.

Set in 16 pt. New Times Roman.

Printed in Great Britain on acid-free paper.

British Library Cataloguing in Publication Data available

Library of Congress Cataloging-in-Publication Data

Mackie, Mary.
    Pamela / by Mary Mackie.
        p.   (large print)   cm.
    ISBN 0–7862–2308–1 (lg. print : sc : alk. paper)
    1. Large type books. I. Title.
    PR6063.A2454 M33   2000
    823'.914—dc21   99–049387

As the milkfloat hummed and rattled around Butterford village, Alfred Davies kept an anxious eye on the thunderclouds gathering over the moors. He hoped the rain would keep off until he finished his round. He had his plastic mac bundled in the cab, but he was wearing open sandals and if there was a downpour he would be bound to get his feet soaked and then Sheila would create. The thought made him grin to himself.

He was a simple man, content with his lot. He enjoyed his job, being in the open air and meeting people, stopping occasionally for a chat and a cup of tea, though so far he hadn't come across any of the man-hungry housewives who were supposed to enliven a milkman's working day. They were old biddies, most of them. The young ones were either out at work or knee-deep in kids. Though Alfred knew that if he did get an invitation to a bit of hanky-panky he'd as like as not turn and run for it.

There was Mrs. Lane, of course, the young widow who lived all by herself in the lonely cottage at Wood End, but she obviously never thought of him as anything but a useful menial. Her father had been stinking rich, so everybody said, but if that was so why then, Alfred wondered, did she still stay at that cottage now that her husband was dead? Her step-mother lived in style at the Hall, further up the valley, but according to rumour there was no love lost between the two. Rumours abounded about Mrs. Lane. She was a puzzle. Alfred had heard all sorts of things about her, but with him such gossip went in one ear and out the other. Speak as you find, was his motto. Pamela Lane had always been pleasant enough to him, in her way. As far as Alfred was concerned, her only fault lay in her failure to pay her bill on time. At the moment she owed him for nearly three weeks.

The sky was growing darker as he approached Wood End Lane, the clouds broiling as they piled rapidly towards the sun and shut it off. When he turned into the lane with its tall trees on either side forming an archway across the road it was so dark he had to switch on his headlights.

The float buzzed happily at its usual leisurely pace. Wood End Cottage was his last call. He hoped the rain would stay away a few minutes longer.

And then another sound joined the gentle whirr of his motor, the sound of a car engine. He was aware of the pale shape of the vehicle rushing towards him through the gloom in the lane. Its headlights flipped on suddenly, blinding him, and he twisted his wheel to the left as the car swept uncomfortably close, sending a blast of cool air through the open door of the cab. The float ran into the verge, tilting slightly. He slammed on the brakes and leapt out, cursing after the fast-disappearing tail-lights of the road hog.

Luckily the float wasn't damaged and the bottles in the back, mostly empty, had stayed intact as far as he could see in that bad light. But a couple of feet more and he would have been in the ditch. Still swearing to himself, he climbed back into the cab and set it in motion as the first roll of thunder muttered across the invisible hills.

A few moments later he was pulling up at the end of the lane, opposite the cottage. From here, only a rough track led into the woods. Few people ever came there. He wondered again why Pamela Lane didn't leave this isolated place and go back to the Hall with her step-mother.

Reaching for the single pint that was her usual order, he glanced at the cottage and froze in surprise, his hand hovering over the crate. In the darkness of the approaching storm the light in the cottage was bright. But it was a red light, flickering. He saw a tongue of flame lick up to the ceiling.

He ran, hardly noticing the lightning that flared over the woods. The thunder-clap came as he reached the back door.

He could see across the colourful kitchen to the living-room, could see the woman lying there, her head and shoulders alarmingly near the flames that were creeping across the carpet. He didn't stop to think. Holding his breath against the smoke and heat, he grabbed Mrs. Lane by the ankles and dragged her unceremoniously into the kitchen.

She was out cold. Her long hair was singed at one side and he had to beat at her arm because the jacket of her suit was smoking. Coughing, he ran water over his handkerchief and strapped it across his nose and mouth, then filled the bowl in the sink with water and went to sling it onto the flames. A log must have dropped out of the fire onto the hearthrug. As yet it had not spread far.

It never occurred to him to go for help. He felt a peculiar kind of exhilaration as he threw more and more water on to the fire. The small settee went up in flames, sending off fumes that made him choke, but after that he had it contained.

For good measure he threw a final bowlful of water onto the grate, putting out every trace of fire in the room. Then he stumbled, coughing, eyes streaming, out of the smoke and fume-filled room and shut the door on the mess, going to stand at the back door and gulp in great draughts of fresh air. A cold wind had risen, blowing the big drops of rain onto his hot face.

Mrs. Lane hadn't stirred. Alfred knelt beside the young woman, gently turning her onto her back. At first he thought she was dead. He gazed in fascinated horror at the

4

great bleeding lump on her head, at the pale, pretty face with long golden lashes and bloodless mouth, the fair hair trailing across it. Then he saw that she was breathing shallowly, her breast rising and falling gently beneath the white blouse and the unbuttoned jacket.

'Mrs. Lane!' he whispered urgently.

When there was no response he leapt up and sprinted out, careless of the slow, heavy raindrops that spat down from the sky. He turned the milkfloat in a rapid U-turn that set all the bottles clattering and sent it back down the lane at top speed, filled with a sense of excitement. He had been at the centre of this. He, Alfred Davies, milkman and professed coward, had put out a fire and saved a woman's life. Although he was shaking with reaction he was looking forward to telling Sheila all about it.

He stopped the float by the nearest telephone box, almost a mile from Wood End Cottage, and had the intense pleasure of dialling 999.

CHAPTER ONE

They drugged me. They had to. Finding myself with no past, no identity, sent me into screaming panic. Who am I? Who?

'There was an accident,' they said soothingly, calm in their white caps and aprons, their white coats. 'A fire at your cottage. You fell. Don't worry.'

Don't worry.

Don't worry.

But who am I?

'You are Pamela Lane,' they told me at last. 'Your neighbours in Butterford know you. Don't worry. It's only temporary. It will come back.'

Pamela Lane. I am Pamela Lane, I told myself. But who *is* Pamela Lane?

'You're a widow. You live alone, at Wood End Cottage. You were very lucky. It might have been a lot worse.'

How could it be worse? I didn't remember a thing. Whatever they told me, it was only words. Inside my head I was nobody.

'Good news!' the Sister said brightly. 'We've contacted your family. Your step-mother will be coming this afternoon. There now, didn't I tell you not to worry? Come along, take these tablets.'

The drugs did help. They made me numb.

                    *   *   *

She was small, this woman who said she was
my step-mother, plumpish, homely, grey-
haired. She looked kind, but her smile was
tentative, even a little apprehensive.

'The Sister has explained it all to me, my
dear. You don't know me, do you? But you
mustn't worry. Your memory will come back in
its own good time. Meanwhile, I want you to
come back to the Hall with me. I'll be glad to
take care of you until you're better. You know
you can't possibly go back to the cottage yet.
What do you say?'

'The Hall?' I managed in the husky croak
that was my voice. 'Is that where you live? I'm
sorry, I can't . . .'

'You can't remember,' she put in swiftly, a
sympathetic hand coming out to touch mine
where it lay on the bed-spread. But just as
swiftly she withdrew the contact, looking
guilty, as though I might have objected to her
touch. 'It doesn't matter, my dear. I do
understand. Yes, the Hall—Butterford Hall—
is where I live with Bevis. Bevis is my son, your
step-brother. Look, they told me not to
confuse you with too many facts but to let
nature take its course. One can't force
amnesia. That's what the doctor said, and
you're still not feeling well, I know, but . . .
Will you come?'

8

'I can't stay here for ever,' I said hoarsely.

'No. No, that's right. So we'll come and collect you tomorrow afternoon. I'll get your old room ready for you—the corner room with the view of the moors. We're looking forward very much to having you home. I really mean that, Pamela.' She glanced at my hand, as if wondering whether to touch it again, but apparently thought better of it and began to back towards the door. 'Goodbye for now, dear. Take care of yourself. And don't worry.'

'Thank you for coming,' I said. 'Oh please . . . what do I call you?'

Her expression puzzled me. She looked to be on the verge of tears. 'You used to call me . . .' She paused, and made it, 'Marjorie. My name's Marjorie. See you tomorrow.'

That wasn't the full truth, I thought, but the tranquillisers wouldn't let me think about it too deeply. I shut my eyes and tried to force my mind back through the blank wall in my memory, but the effort only exhausted me. I couldn't even remember the woman herself. She might never have existed until she stepped into my room just now, as I myself seemed to have had no existence before two days ago, when I had woken up in this hospital bed.

Pamela Lane, I said in my head. You are Pamela Lane. But it was just a name, a stranger's name. I lifted my left hand and looked at the gold wedding-ring that slipped easily up and down on the third finger. Surely I

9

should remember the man who had given it to me? But there was nothing, only the wall of forgetfulness, like an impenetrable mist.

The following afternoon I sat on the bed dressed in the clothes my step-mother had brought from the cottage—a wide flared skirt that was loose around the waist, a shirt blouse, hand-knitted sweater, and a navy-blue showerproof coat that had seen better days. The attire did not help my morale.

Marjorie Ennis came in with the ward sister and a big, fair-haired man in his thirties who swept up my suitcase without more than a cursory glance at me.

'Bevis,' his mother said appealingly, at which he turned cold grey eyes in my direction and inclined his head, saying flatly, 'Pamela. Good afternoon.'

There was such unfriendliness in his manner that I, perplexed by it, made no reply.

'Are you ready, dear?' Marjorie Ennis asked with a bright smile that was intended to make up for her son's abrupt behaviour. 'Come along. The car's just outside the main door.'

Saying my goodbyes to the Sister, I sent a last longing glance around the bright room which was the only home I could remember. I had to choke back the desperate urge to let my panic show itself. Butterford Hall was just a name to me. It brought to mind no picture. And these people might as well be total strangers, this cold-eyed man and the anxious woman who was making such an effort to be kind.

She insisted that I should sit beside Bevis, so that I should have a better view of the countryside, then told me that her son had been to my cottage that morning to make sure all was secure, so I had nothing to worry about.

'Thank you,' I said to the silent man at my side, but the only reply was a bitter, tight-lipped glance.

'Is there much damage?' I asked. It seemed an appropriate question.

'Quite a bit,' Bevis said unhelpfully.

After a moment his mother added, 'The main room's a dreadful mess, I'm afraid, but the milkman who found you managed to put out the blaze before it spread too far. Were you insured?—Oh, of course, you won't know. I'm sorry. But we'll find out about that. And you mustn't worry. Any help you need, Bevis and I will be only too glad . . .'

Her son made a short, derisive sound that cut her off. She lapsed into silence and when I glanced at Bevis he was grim-faced, concentrating on the road.

We were climbing away from the town, up a long road that occcasionally took a sharp turn. There were bleak hills ahead, with cloud shadows chasing across them. As far as I could remember I had never seen the place before.

'Is the cottage far from Butterford Hall?' I asked.

'Five miles,' Bevis replied. 'Why?'

'I was wondering if it was within walking distance.'

'Yes, it is,' he said drily. 'With a strong pair of shoes and a head for heights there's a short-cut. But you're not one for hill-walking, Pamela.'

'Oh,' I said. 'Aren't I?'

'Bevis!' Marjorie said sharply, and I saw him smile to himself in bitter amusement.

Bevis didn't like me. I suppose I had known that from the moment I saw him. Perhaps the feeling was mutual, if only I could remember. He had certainly not endeared himself to me in the short time I seemed to have known him.

We reached the moorland tops and followed the snaking road until we turned off down a steep incline into a tree-filled cleft of a valley which eventually opened out into pleasant meadowland where cows grazed. The car slowed and turned in between gates almost hidden at the edge of a wood, threading its way beneath dappled sunlight, between trees lush with late summer, slowly climbing again.

The house came abruptly into sight, a solid mansion of grey stone fronted by sloping lawns with round flowerbeds. In front of the house a single massive oak spread its branches as the car drew up.

'Well?' Bevis demanded.

Startled, I looked round and found him glowering at me. 'I'm sorry. What . . .'

12

'Nothing clicked yet? No light in the darkness?'

'No.' I shook my head. 'No, I'm afraid not.'

'It really doesn't matter,' his mother put in pleadingly. 'We mustn't rush her, Bevis. They told us . . .'

Before she had finished the sentence he was out of the car, going to take my case from the boot. As Mrs Ennis and I left the vehicle another woman appeared from the house, coming eagerly to greet us. She smiled, but her eyes were sharp in her thin face.

'This is Phyllis Franklin,' my step-mother told me, 'my very good friend who helps me in the house, and keeps me company.'

'Pleased to meet you,' the woman said, shaking hands. 'You do look pale, poor thing. Come along in. Your room's all ready and I'll soon have some tea made.'

There was an impression of warmth and space in the house. Flowers glowed in every available corner, with shining brass ornaments reflecting in polished woodwork. Our feet made no sound on the deep carpet as the two women conducted me up the stairs to an airy, pleasant room with white furniture and a large bay window set across the corner.

I was aware that they were both watching me, waiting for my reaction, but the room was as strange to me as everything else.

'It's very nice,' I said. 'Thank you.'

'You'll want to get settled in,' Marjorie said

softly, stifling a sigh. 'We'll have some tea in about half an hour. Will you come down, or would you prefer to rest quietly?'

'If you don't mind,' I replied, putting a hand to my aching head, 'I think I'll have a nap. I don't feel as well as I might.'

'I'll bring her a cup of tea straight away,' Phyllis suggested. 'She looks as though she ought to be in bed, just out of hospital and all.'

When they had gone I noticed my suitcase standing by the door. Bevis must have brought it up. My head was spinning as I sat down on the bed, my fingers exploring my short, silky hair and the plaster stuck over the painful lump on my temple. They had had to cut my hair to attend to the contusion and it had looked such a mess, straggly and smoke-filled, that I had asked for the hairdresser, who had chopped off my tresses, carefully washed what was left, and blow-dried it into what she said was the latest style. I was pleased with the result, though I couldn't remember what I had looked like before. Even the face which looked back at me from the mirror had been the face of a stranger, pale, big-eyed.

Pamela Lane. My name is Pamela Lane.

Discovering that I was trying to force my memory again, I went to the bedroom window and knelt on the seat. There was the promised view of the moors, rocky hills rising beyond the tree-tops. How often had I sat at this window, and how long ago? Before my marriage?

With a tap on the door Phyllis Franklin came in bringing me a small pot of tea and a plate of biscuits. She placed the tray on the bedside table and put on a smile that didn't alter the watchful, speculative look in her eyes.

'It can't be very nice not remembering anything. Does it all seem strange?'

'Yes, I'm afraid so,' I replied. 'It's ridiculous, but I don't remember Marjorie or Bevis, or you. Not even the house, or the countryside.'

She came to stand by me, smoothing her sensible apron over her plain skirt. 'You wouldn't remember me, anyway. We never met. I've only been here three years. Marjorie and I were friends at school and always kept in touch, so when I wrote and told her my husband was retiring and looking for a little part-time job to keep him occupied, she asked us to come here. She was very lonely after your father died, you know, and she didn't want Bevis to feel tied to her, so it was an ideal arrangement for us all. Albert and me have our own little flat on the ground floor at the back. He does the garden and I help out in the house. We love it. And it's all thanks to Marjorie. She's the kindest person on earth. You're lucky to have her.'

'Yes, I'm very grateful to her, but ...' Puzzled, I looked up at her sallow face with its deep lines round the eyes and mouth and saw that same hard expression. 'You've been here three years, and yet we've never met?'

'That's right. You've never visited her once. Far be it from me to criticise, but don't you think that's a bit unkind? I don't know what started it and I don't want to know. Marjorie usually tells me everything, but that's one subject she won't talk about. She wouldn't say a bad thing about anybody, but after what she's done . . .'

'You forget,' I said quietly. 'I don't know what happened myself. As far as I remember, I never saw Marjorie before yesterday. From what I know of her, I can't imagine what quarrel there might have been, but Bevis . . . You may be right. There is something. Are you sure you've no idea what it might be?'

'All she said was that she hadn't seen much of you since you'd been married. She told me I wasn't to mention it. She wants you to have the chance for a whole new start. But she's been a good friend to me and I don't like seeing her hurt. She's very easily hurt. You'd do well to remember that. It's because she cares too much about people. She cares about *you*, no matter how you've treated her. It's only through her goodness that you're here. I heard them arguing yesterday. If it had been up to Bevis you wouldn't have come here at all.'

'I rather gathered he wasn't too pleased with the arrangement,' I said. 'But at the moment all I feel is gratitude—to both of them. Without them I'd really be in limbo.'

'As long as you remember that,' Phyllis said

16

darkly, and left me.

I lay on the bed, my thoughts whirling. Yes, I was grateful, but perhaps I ought not to be here. If the feud between us was that bad, would I live to regret my acceptance of Marjorie's kindness? There was so much I wanted to know, so much that ought to be there in my mind, but there was nothing. I felt like a stranger here, knowing nothing of the people, their thoughts and feelings, their history. The tension of the day dissolved itself in tears of frustration and I slept.

It was dark when I woke, to the fresh panic of not knowing who or where I was. It took a moment to remember that I was Pamela Lane and this was Butterford Hall. I reached out for the lamp and switched it on, looking round at the room. My case still stood where Bevis had left it, but the tea-tray was gone.

Dragging myself off the bed, I opened the wardrobe and found, to my surprise, several long evening dresses and three pairs of high-heeled sandals. Had I left them there when I moved to the cottage? Why?

I turned to the case, opening it on the bed and taking out the three pairs of jeans, the assortment of loose blouses, a couple of jumpers, underwear, plus the multi-coloured woven poncho that was fraying in places. Clearly I had little money and lived a simple life, if these clothes were anything to go by. The contents of the suitcase were in startling contrast to the glamorous dresses in the wardrobe.

Coming back from the bathroom refreshed by a wash, I found Marjorie standing in the doorway to my room surveying the disorder I had created.

'I heard you moving about,' she said. 'How are you feeling now?'

'Better, thank you. I'm sorry about the mess. I had just started unpacking.' I began folding the scattered clothes, putting them into drawers.

'You always were untidy,' Marjorie said fondly. 'Pamela . . . it's good to have you home. I really mean that.'

Pausing with the tatty poncho in my hands, I looked at her. 'I know you do. You're very kind, Marjorie.'

'Not kind. It's what mothers are for. And—I hate to say it, but . . . those clothes aren't very pretty. Perhaps we could go shopping together. Families are meant to help each other. If only you had let us know . . . I know what it is, of course. Pride. But you shouldn't be too proud to turn to us, Pamela. We're your family. Your father was very good to Bevis and me. He always wanted you to share what we had. If only . . .' She stopped, seeing by my face that I wasn't following her, and added with a sigh, 'I'm sorry, my dear. It's very difficult, seeing you standing there the same as you always were. Just . . . let me do things for you. It's

18

what I want, what your father would have wanted. We can be friends, can't we?'

'Weren't we friends before?' I asked.

'Not exactly.' Giving me a small, sad smile, she walked across the room and drew the curtains against the night outside. 'It's quite mild this evening, isn't it? But if you aren't warm enough there are extra blankets in the chest. This time of year it can turn cold very suddenly. It's almost October.'

'Yes, I know. Marjorie . . . those dresses in the wardrobe . . .'

'You remember them?' When I shook my head she went on rapidly, 'Well, it doesn't matter, dear. They said we must be patient. All that really matters is that you're safe, here with us. You're home where you belong.'

'Bevis doesn't seem very pleased about it,' I observed, which made Marjorie flush and busy herself straightening the bed-covers.

'He'll come round,' she assured me. 'Give him time. He feels the same way I do, underneath. It's just . . . well, we won't go into that. There's no point in raking over the past.'

'I *have* no past,' I said. 'None that I remember. And I *want* to know, whatever the doctors said about taking it slowly. Can you imagine how frightening it is, not to know the first thing about yourself? Oh—the basics I know, but none of the details. What sort of person am I? What have I been doing these past . . .' I leaned against the dressing-table,

19

feeling that my head was about to burst. 'You see! I don't even know how old I am!'

'You're twenty-seven. Twenty-eight next month. My dear . . .' She came towards me as if to comfort me, but stopped herself and let her hands drop to her sides helplessly. 'It's difficult for me, too. You were always so sure of yourself and now you seem so . . . so vulnerable. If only you knew how often I've wanted to be close to you. I never had a daughter of my own.' Tears came into her eyes as she stood there looking at me. 'Oh, Pamela! If only we could go back and start again.'

'Perhaps we can,' I said. 'Not go back, but start all over. Whatever I did to hurt you, Marjorie, I'm sorry. I can't believe I ever meant to be hurtful.'

Suddenly she couldn't hold back any longer. She came and put her arms about me, saying through her tears, 'You didn't, darling. You were young, and bitterly unhappy, and stubborn, and very very proud. But that's all done with now. We'll be friends from now on.' Stepping away, she looked up at me with a tremuluous smile. 'Won't we?'

'Of course,' I said unsteadily, the light glittering through my own tears.

'Of course,' she repeated, taking my hand and patting it. 'Now, what I came to ask you was about a meal. Do you want it here, or will you have it on a tray in the sitting-room?'

'Is Bevis in?' I asked.

'No, he's gone out with his girlfriend. We had our dinner some time ago. But ... don't let him upset you. You can't go on avoiding each other. There was a time when you two were very good friends. If we all try to live amicably together ... Anyway, you'll come down, will you? Good.'

The sitting-room was large, decorated in autumnal shades of brown and orange, and dominated by a stone chimney column with wide archways either side leading to the dining-room. I sat in one of the deeply-buttoned arm-chairs while Marjorie rested with her feet up on the settee. Three big table lamps strategically placed about the room provided light as I ate my meal.

'It's a lovely house,' I commented.

'Yes, it is. Much grander than I ever thought *I* would live in.'

'How long have you been here?'

'Since I married your father, seven years ago.'

I was surprised. 'Not long, then.'

'No, not very long. We only had four years ... He made the alterations himself, with help from his men. He was a master builder.'

'Tell me about him,' I begged.

She looked at me doubtfully. 'There's so much. Where shall I begin? Pamela ... I do think it would be best to let it come back gradually, you know.'

'Why? Are there things you'd rather not tell me? About my father?'

'Oh no!' Stiffly swinging her legs down, as though they were aching, she sat forward earnestly. 'Your father was a dear, kind man—and clever, too. He built up that business with his own hands. Look . . . If you like, I'll tell you the gist of the story, what I know of it. Oh . . . leave that tray in the hearth for now.'

I put down the empty tray and curled up in the chair, ready to listen, to hear some of the things that my mind had blocked out. Her grey head bent over her hands, Marjorie thought for a moment before breaking the silence.

'You were born in Cannonfield—the town where you were in hospital. You lived in a house . . . I'll show it to you some time. There was your father and mother, and you, of course, and a brother. He'd have been about Bevis's age if he'd lived. His name was Peter and he wanted to be in the Army, but when he was sixteen he went on an expedition with some other cadets and they got caught in a snowstorm in the mountains. Three of them died. I'm afraid Peter was one of the three.

'Anyway, my first husband was at that time working for your father. He was a painter and plasterer. We'd just moved to Cannonfield from Hull. And when I heard about Peter I just had to call on your parents and tell them how sorry I was. I knew how I'd have felt, if it had been Bevis . . .' She paused, remembering, emotion tautening her face. 'What was I saying?'

'About my brother?'

'Oh, yes. Well, shortly after that I lost my husband very suddenly. He was only ill for a short while before ... Anyway, your father was very kind to me. He helped me get sorted out—I was in a fair old state, away from my family and friends and nobody to turn to—and when things were settling down again he used to drop in occasionally to see how we were getting along. He was very interested in Bevis, and Bevis thought the world of him. Frank—your father—always used to say that it made up, in a way, for losing Peter.' She paused, glancing at me worriedly. 'I promise you, your mother knew all about it. She used to send me clothes that she'd finished with, and things for Bevis that she came across. There was nothing ... like that, between your father and me until after your mother died, and by then we'd become such friends it only seemed natural that we should join the two families together.'

'How old was I at the time?' I asked.

'You were just turned twenty when your mother died. Mind you, she'd been ill for a long time. Your father knew she'd never get well again, but he kept it from you. I expect that's why it came as a bit of a shock, when it happened. You wouldn't seem to accept it. And when your father married me, you ... well, let's say you were too young to understand.'

23

'You mean—I didn't approve?'

'No, my dear, indeed you didn't,' Marjorie sighed. 'I can't tell you how glad I am to be able to tell you my side of it, calmly. You never would let me explain how things were. We had a difficult time of it until you met David and went off to live with him at his cottage.'

I turned the loose weding-ring round on my finger. 'David?' My voice was subdued. So his name had been David, had it? David Lane. Not even that stirred my memory. 'What happened to him?'

'He was killed, on the motorway. His lorry overturned. But even then you wouldn't let me help you. You refused to see me when I came, and sent back my letters unopened. Oh, my dear, whatever happens, don't let us go back to being enemies. Surely, after all we've both been through . . .' She sighed again. 'Time will tell, I suppose.'

'What was he like—David?' I asked.

Marjorie shook her head sadly. 'I never met him. You wouldn't bring him home to meet us. One day you just packed your bags and announced that you were going to live with him. There was nothing we could do about it. We only knew you'd been married because of the announcement in the paper. Your father came to visit you a few times, but he and David didn't get on very well. And then . . .' Her voice dropped. 'He died, too.'

'My father?'

'They said it was a heart attack. He left here fit and healthy one morning, to go to Manchester for a business meeting, and . . .', She fished a handkerchief from her sleeve and blew her nose. 'I do miss him, Pamela. You'll never know how happy we were those four years. Of course he left me well provided for, but that's not the same as having him here. We got on so well, liked the same things. Oh, it wasn't all romantic like it is when you're young, but we were contented together. If only . . .' Another sigh escaped her. 'That's life, I suppose.'

I watched her for a moment, trying to think myself into the story she had told me, but remembering that it was told from *her* point of view, not mine. There must have been reasons for the way I had behaved. The picture she painted of me was not a pleasant one.

'I wouldn't have blamed you if you had left me in that hospital,' I said at length.

A sad smile curved her mouth. 'How could I do that, my dear? If only for your father's sake . . . This is where you belong. There have been misunderstandings in the past, but they're all over now. Let's concentrate on doing better in the future.'

*   *   *

I slept long and deeply in that corner room at Butterford Hall and woke feeling physically stronger and mentally alert, but for that barrier across my memory. I still felt like a stranger here, but refused to let myself give way to despair. It would come. Give it time.

It was a golden morning, sunlight lying across the moors and patches of yellow beginning to show in the trees. Since I had little choice of what to wear I put on a pair of jeans and one of my loose blouses and went down to the dining-room, where Marjorie and Bevis were breakfasting.

'Oh, good morning,' Marjorie greeted brightly. 'I thought you might want to lie in today. How are you feeling?'

'Fine,' I assured her.

'What would you like for breakfast?' my step-mother asked, leaving her seat. 'Egg and bacon? Or there's some smoked haddock, or . . .'

'Nothing, thank you,' I interrupted with a laugh. 'I never eat . . .' I stopped, astonished. 'Good heavens! I was going to say "I never eat breakfast". It feels to be true. That's a good sign, isn't it?'

'Wonderful!' Marjorie exclaimed. 'Sit down, Pamela. You'll at least have some coffee, won't you? What would you like to do today?'

I had already thought about that. 'I'd like to go to the cottage. Just to see it. There might be something that will jog my memory. You never know.'

'I'll lay odds on it,' Bevis said in an

undertone, not looking up.

Marjorie and I both stared at him in bewilderment, but he didn't explain further or take any more notice of us. But something about his voice had made a cold shiver run up my spine. Why did he hate me so?

'Anyway,' I added to fill the awkward silence, 'I ought to see what needs doing, didn't I?'

'Of course,' Marjorie agreed. 'If that's what you want to do, Bevis will take you. I don't think you ought to be alone too much at the moment. I'd come myself, but I'm going to church with Phyllis and Albert.'

'And I,' said Bevis, carefully setting down his empty cup, 'have arranged to play tennis. So Pamela will just have to wait, won't she?'

'Bevis, please . . .' his mother appealed. 'You promised me . . .'

His head came up, revealing the anger on his face. 'I promised I'd be civil. I will be civil. But I'm damned if I'll put myself out to go ferrying her all over the countryside. I'm sorry, mother.'

'I think that's most uncharitable of you,' Marjorie said hotly. 'Excuse me. I'll make a fresh pot of coffee.'

She left an uncomfortable silence in the room.

'I wouldn't dream of interfering with your plans,' I said in a small voice. 'I can always walk. You did say that was possible.'

Very slowly, he turned his head to look at me with sceptical grey eyes. 'I did, but you have to know the way or you'd get lost. Not that that would bother me, but it might worry mother and you've already caused her too many sleepless nights.'

'So it seems,' I said quietly. 'From what she told me . . . I can understand, partly, why you dislike me. Will it make any difference if I tell you I'm sorry, genuinely sorry, for whatever I've done?'

'And your being sorry makes everything all right, does it?' he asked heavily. 'The way you treated my mother, and your father, not to mention your attitude to me. Do you seriously think all that can be mended by an apology?'

I met his eyes levelly, knowing I was near to tears. 'If I could remember, I'd try to make amends for each and every thing. I don't want to be at odds with you.'

'Oh, for God's sake!' He swung out of his chair and stood glaring at me across the table. 'You can stop putting on *that* act. It might fool mother, but I'm not so gullible, or so trusting. I know exactly what's going to happen. You'll go to the cottage. You'll suddenly have a brainstorm and get your memory back, and everything will be peachy. You'll have got your way without having to crawl, won't you?'

Swallowing a lump in my throat, I stared at him stupidly. 'I don't know what you mean. You'll have to explain.'

'Explain!' he exploded, then suddenly leaned on the table, speaking slowly and clearly, intense fury burning in his eyes. 'I don't believe you, Pamela. I don't believe you have amnesia. If you really want to know what I think—I think you staged the whole thing, knowing that my mother would come running to your aid.'

'That isn't true,' I said in a low voice.

'Isn't it? Well, we'll see. But it's all mightily convenient, isn't it? For you, that is. But I'll tell you one thing—you're going to have to be a very good actress to carry it off, better than you were in "The Fawn".'

' "The Fawn"?' I echoed.

'Perhaps you thought I'd forgotten your efforts at amateur drama. That's what gave you the idea, wasn't it? You were pretty good as that poor lost amnesiac girl in the play, but then you only had to remember the lines. This is real. You'll slip up sooner or later. It almost happened just now, when you forgot to forget that you don't eat breakfast.'

This unjustified accusation only bewildered me. 'I only wish you were right, Bevis. I assure you it's all too horribly real. What on earth makes you think I'd go to such lengths to deceive you? What can I possibly gain?'

Bevis sat down again, smiling unpleasantly. 'Do you think I can't guess why all this is happening? You must think I'm stupid, Pamela. I know as well as you do that the five

29

years are nearly up. And my mother isn't a young woman. What if something was to happen to her before the end of the five years? It must have been preying on your mind. Not even you would throw away your inheritance, whatever crazy ideas that husband of yours instilled in you.'

I stared at him, puzzled. 'I still don't know what you're talking about. Five years? Inheritance?'

It was then that Marjorie spoke from the doorway, her voice shaking. 'I'll never forgive you for this, Bevis. To accuse Pamela of . . .'

'Of shamming,' Bevis said, and closed his mouth like a trap, glaring narrowly at me.

Marjorie carefully placed the coffee pot on the table. She stood with her head high, her face pale, addressing me calmly despite the tremor in her voice. 'In your father's will, he left everything to me during my lifetime. When I'm gone, everything is to be shared equally between you and Bevis, on condition that friendly relations have been restored within five years of your father's death. If not, Bevis will inherit all there is.'

'And there are just eighteen months to go before your time runs out,' Bevis added with satisfaction.

CHAPTER TWO

It seemed that I was an heiress, but all I could do was look blankly at the grim face of my step-brother. None of it had any meaning for me. I couldn't remember ever having a father, much less quarrelling with him. They might as well have been talking about someone else.

'I really don't know how you can!' Marjorie cried. 'You're not being fair, Bevis. Pamela would never . . .'

'I know her better than you do,' Bevis interrupted.

'Even so! Surely you're not going to say she deliberately knocked herself out? Look at that dressing on her head. They had to cut her hair to clean up the cut. It's not possible for her to have done it on purpose.'

'Maybe not,' he agreed dubiously, his eyes on my face, 'It's still a convenient thing to have happened. If I'm wrong, I'm sorry, but you can't blame me for being suspicious after the way . . . if we get a move on I can take you to the cottage before I pick Lorraine up. Are you ready?'

'Just about,' I said.

Marjorie put her hand on my shoulder, keeping me in my seat. 'You're not going until you've had some coffee. Lorraine will wait.'

Perhaps the doctors had been right about

taking it slowly. I was now totally confused, trying to remember everything I had learned and trying to understand what lay behind it. When Bevis and I drove away from Butterford Hall there were a hundred questions I wanted to ask, but each time one of them was on the tip of my tongue I hesitated for fear he should think I was faking. I couldn't face his sarcasm again so soon. I needed time to think.

We drove along the sunny dale and through the pretty village of Butterford, turning down a narrow lane with trees either side reaching out to touch branches across the road. Perhaps half a mile later the lane petered out into a rough track leading up into the woods. It was here that Bevis stopped. On our right there was a sturdy little cottage almost hidden behind banks of flowering shrubs. It was very quiet but for the singing of birds, and very isolated. All around the woods crowded close.

'Remember it?' Bevis demanded.

I shook my head. 'I could swear I'd never been here before. Believe me!'

He studied my face for a moment before saying, 'I'm beginning to. Do you want to get out, or . . .'

'That's why I came.'

'I promised to meet Lorraine at half past,' he said with a frown and a significant glance at the car clock, which showed twenty minutes past ten. 'Will you be long?'

'I don't know. Does Lorraine live far away?'

'Far enough.'

'Then ... could you come back for me later?'

With a sigh of exasperation he began to beat an impatient tattoo on the driving wheel. 'You always expect the world to revolve around you. I can't possibly get back before twelve thirty, and if Lorraine has other plans she'll be furious.'

'Then why did you bring me?'

'Because I'm not having you cause trouble between me and my mother! That's why! All right, I'll come back in a couple of hours.'

'Thank you.' Without further ado I climbed from the car and crossed the road to the cottage gate. It had been painted in rainbow stripes, though the paint was now peeling badly. A shrill creak disturbed the quietness as I pushed it open and I paused, my heart suddenly pumping in alarm. The cottage lay so still and deserted, with only the woods for company. A few days ago I had narrowly escaped death here.

'Pamela!' Bevis was leaning out of the car window, holding out a key. 'You'll need this, won't you?'

As I returned to take the key he looked at me with narrowed eyes. 'Are you sure you'll be all right? Perhaps I shouldn't leave you here. Let me take you back to . . .'

'No! No, now I'm here I want to face it. Don't worry about me.'

'Face what?' Bevis asked.

My head shook convulsively. 'I don't know. Whatever it is that I had to forget, maybe. The longer I put it off, the harder it will be. You go. I'll be all right.'

'Well, if you're sure,' he said, and started the engine.

I stood at the gate watching as the white Viva turned and drove away, leaving me alone with the birds and the trees—and my forgotten home. When the noise of the vehicle had died away along the long green tunnel of the lane I turned once more to the cottage, trying to find something familiar about it. But it remained strange, even when I trod down the gravel path and put the key into the lock.

The key wouldn't go in properly. Stooping down, I saw that there was already a key on the inside. It must be the back door key that I had in my hand.

Making my way past a group of towering hollyhocks at the corner of the cottage, I soon found myself in the back yard. A couple of ancient sheds leaned on each other for support. There was a brick path between them and the back door, where a stone tub full of flowers held court over an array of old saucers and plates lying on the ground. Flies buzzed around the dishes, emphasising the stillness, while beyond the sheds there was a neat vegetable patch with barely a weed in sight between the rows. The whole area was separated from the woods by a low, rickety wooden fence.

This is mine, I thought firmly. I like gardening, obviously. I planted those vegetables, hoed the weeds and ate the produce. But it was with a lump in my throat that I approached the door and this time turned the key.

The kitchen was clean, gay with colours, but there were few modern conveniences. The sink was made of stone, supported on bricks, the aperture beneath covered by a bright curtain matching those at the window. Three chairs, pink, yellow and blue, stood by an old table covered in flowered Formica and there was a small grate in the corner with a hand-painted screen across it. But at least there was electricity, feeding the small cooker and a fridge that hummed gently to itself.

The smell of burning lay stale on the air. I walked across to the inner door and lifted the latch, forcing myself to enter the next room.

It was here that the fire had been, spreading from the hearthrug. The wall around the fireplace was blackened. A great hole in the carpet showed charred floorboards beneath and a small couch was just a charcoal skeleton. Overhead, scorch marks had left brown patches on the ceiling and everywhere there was evidence of the water that had been used to put out the flames, plus that bitter, throat-catching smell.

It wasn't as bad as I had expected, but I couldn't picture the room as it used to be. It didn't feel like my home. It felt alien, even hostile.

Still hoping for something to jog my memory, I ventured through a door in the near corner. It led into a long, gloomy hallway with a front door at the far end. Beneath the stairs was a cupboard holding coats, shoes and a vacuum cleaner, while another door led into what was clearly a workroom.

A sewing machine held pride of place, with scraps of material lying about and an untidy pile of patterns. With stupid hot tears in my eyes I went listlessly round the room, examining the embroidery work that lay discarded. In a little cupboard there were jumbled tubes of oil paint and a tall jar for holding brushes. I was artistic, it seemed.

Distressed by my continued disability to remember, I fled from that room and went upstairs to the three bed-rooms, only one of which had been in use. The other two were piled with odds and ends in boxes. On the dresser in the largest room, where a double bed was carelessly made, I found a photograph of a man with tousled dark hair and an engaging grin.

David, I thought as I picked up the frame. It must be David, I stared down at the face of the stranger who had been my husband, a great sadness weighing me down. I had lost him completely now. Lost even the memory of him. It was so damnably frustrating.

Suddenly I could no longer face the strangeness of it all. I put down the photograph and hurried back down the stairs, needing fresh air.

On the threshold of the kitchen I paused in surprise at the sight of three cats prowling there. They all came towards me, mewing plaintively, and I recalled the dishes outside. Were these my cats, then?

'Are you hungry?' I asked them. 'Poor things . . .'

There were tins of catfood in a cupboard and an opener in a drawer—where I had expected it to be. Surely that meant something? Perhaps instinct was coming to my aid. With the cats brushing round my legs I put some food in three of the saucers and watched the lithe animals begin to wolf it down before filling two other dishes with water for them since the milk in the fridge had gone sour. They accepted it all with equanimity, used to such treatment. I must have done the same thing a thousand times.

Bringing a chair to the doorway, I sat in the sun watching the cats wash themselves contentedly. This was my home, I told myself. Here I lived and worked, in the company of these three cats. But it didn't feel like home. I almost expected the real owner to appear and demand to know what I was doing. Stupid.

I glanced at my watch and sighed as I saw that less than half an hour had gone by since Bevis left me there. The place was too quiet for comfort. Sunlight and shadow made strange shapes in the breeze-filled woods and all the time I was aware of that desolated room behind me.

The flesh on the back of my neck began to creep, making me move the chair so that I had my back to the outer wall of the cottage. The solitude made me uneasy. How could I ever have lived here alone? Was there some reason for my apprehension, for the menace that I sensed in this apparently innocent place? Exactly what had happened here four days ago?

No! I sharply stopped myself from following that line of thought. Trying to force my memory only led to despair, and a headache. I would be better employed in constructive thinking.

Going over all that Marjorie had told me, I began to piece together what must have been my motivation for the things I had done. Why, for instance, had I resented my father's second marriage? Probably I had seen it as a betrayal of my own mother. If I had been very close to her, and unable, as Marjorie had said, to accept her death, it might have come as a shock that my father could re-marry so soon. I could imagine the emotional difficulties which would have followed, and the eagerness with

38

which I left Butterford Hall to come to this cottage and the man I loved. I must have resolved to have no more to do with my family.

It seemed that I had kept that resolve, even through the death of my father and my husband. Pride, Marjorie called it. So wasn't I now betraying myself by accepting her hospitality? Or was Bevis right in thinking I had set fire to my own home solely to touch Marjorie's sympathy? Perhaps I had been desperate enough to do it.

I just couldn't remember.

Faintly in the distance I heard the sound of a car. It was coming closer, slowly up the lane. I wondered if Bevis had cut short his tennis session with Lorraine, but remained where I was until the car had stopped outside the cottage and I heard the door slam. Then I rose and went to stand by the corner of the cottage, looking down the side path a little nervously.

My caller brushed past the hollyhocks and stopped on seeing me, a slow smile warming his tanned face. He was a stranger. He looked about the same age as Bevis, and the same height, but he didn't have the breadth of shoulder which made my step-brother look so massive. This man was dark, attractive, dressed in a smart brown suit.

'Hello, Pam,' he said softly.

'Hello,' I returned, feeling unsteady. I put one hand on the wall for support, blinking at him. Did I know him?

We stood staring at each other for what seemed an age, he smiling quizzically as if waiting for me to say more. All at once the world seemed to narrow and grow hazy. I felt my senses slipping, shook my head. Whirling greyness claimed me.

When I came round I was lying on the path with the stranger bending anxiously over me.

'I'd never have come unannounced if I'd known . . .' he said worriedly. 'Can you get up? That's right. Lean on me. Here, sit in this chair.'

He brought me a glass of water and watched me sip it. I felt vaguely sick and my head was thumping. I should never have come here alone.

'I thought it would be a surprise,' the man was saying. 'I never imagined it would be enough of a shock to make you faint. Aren't you well? What have you done to your head?'

'I'm not sure. There was a fire here. I must have fallen. I . . . don't remember anything.'

'About what happened, you mean?'

'About anything. Total amnesia.'

It was his turn to look shocked, eyes very blue against his tan. 'Then what the devil are you doing here alone? Shouldn't you be in hospital?'

'There's nothing physically wrong with me, apart from this bump on my head. They said it would be better for me to be in familiar surroundings. I'm staying at Butterford Hall.

Do you know Butterford Hall?'

'Yes, of course.' He knelt before me, studying my face. 'You mean ... you don't know me?'

'I'm afraid not.'

'It wasn't the sight of me that made you faint?'

'No, I don't think so. I expect I'm trying to do too much too soon. I want so desperately to remember. I thought coming here might help, but it hasn't.'

There was a frown between his brows as he looked up at me, coming to terms with what I had told him.

'Who are you?' I asked, and saw his mouth twist wrily.

'James Summerton,' he said.

I shook my head. 'I'm sorry. It means nothing to me.'

'Don't be sorry. It's not the greeting I expected, but that's not your fault. It's funny. I thought I was prepared for all eventualities, but I'd never imagined ... How did you get here from the Hall?'

'Bevis brought me.'

'And left you alone?' The idea apparently shocked him. 'That's typical of him. I'd have thought by now he would have forgotten about ... Do you want me to take you home'?'

'Oh, no, thank you. He's coming back for me later.'

He asked me about the fire and went to

41

look at the damage, coming back with the comment that it might have been worse.

'How about some coffee?' he suggested. 'No, sit still. I'll make it. Where are the things?'

'I only wish I could tell you,' I said heavily. 'Mr. . . . Summerton, did you say?'

In the doorway he paused and turned, smiling ruefully. 'It's James, actually. You and I were on first-name terms a long time ago.'

'Oh, I'm sorry. But . . . why did you assume I was shocked by the sight of you?'

'Because,' he said slowly, stepping back into the yard, 'it's a good five years since we met. I've been abroad. Only got back recently; When I heard about David I had to come. You may have forgotten me, Pam, but I haven't forgotten you, though I've tried hard enough.'

He held out his hands for mine, drew me out of the chair and slowly took me in his arms, watching my face all the time. My only response was bewildered passivity, even when he let his lips touch mine.

'That's how things were with us once,' he told me as he released me. 'We quarrelled, rather viciously, and I went away with the intention of joining the Foreign Legion, or something equally juvenile. It all seems rather stupid now.'

'Yes,' I said blankly, which made him give me a wry smile as he turned back to the kitchen.

Following him, I filled the kettle while he found cups and a jar of instant coffee. There was sugar in a little blue bowl and in the absence of fresh milk we opened a tin.

He started to say something but stopped, shaking his head. 'I keep wanting to ask you questions. It's very odd. You've hardly changed at all. It's hard to believe that five years have slipped by since . . . You lost your father, too. I'm sorry.'

'Did you know my father?' I asked, sitting at the table, consciously ignoring his flattery.

'Yes. Not that he approved of me. No one was good enough for his only daughter. Except Bevis, of course. He always thought very highly of Bevis, though I often wondered if he'd go so far as to accept him as a son-in-law. It never came to that, of course.'

What he was implying astonished me. 'You mean, Bevis and I . . .'

'You were inseparable all one summer.'

'When?'

James came to sit opposite me, stirring his coffee. 'It must be . . . nine or ten years ago now. He was home from University, doing brilliantly, bronzed and athletic. Your father invited him into the social swim and you took one look and wham! But you were a fickle little thing in those days. Come the autumn you soon forgot about him. That's when you and I began to gel. We lost touch for a while when your mother was so ill, but you came back to me when you knew your father was going to marry his fancy-woman.'

I caught my breath in surprise. 'Fancy-woman? Marjorie?'

'He'd been visiting her for years. You're the only one who didn't seem to know what was going on. Why else did your father take Bevis so much under his wing?'

'But Marjorie said it was an innocent friendship.'

'She would, wouldn't she? I'm sorry, love, perhaps I shouldn't have told you, but you'll remember for yourself one of these days. You were pretty upset about it at the time. It galled you having to live under the same roof.'

'Oh, is *that* why . . .'

'Mind you,' James went on, 'when you look at it objectively, your father was only human. Your mother had been ill for a long time. And at least he did marry the woman as soon as he was free. You can't really blame him. Perhaps now you can see that. When you've been through the mill yourself it's easier to forgive people their weaknesses.'

'Yes. Yes, I suppose so. It was soon afterwards that I met David, was it?'

'David. Yes.' He studied his clasped hands for a moment. 'I didn't think he was your type, but then I was jealous. And I went away in a huff before I knew how things turned out.'

'And what 'type' was David?' I asked.

'A rebel. A rabid-left-winger. He dropped

out of University to become a lorry-driver. He'd seen the light and was going to change the world. After you met him you used to come out with the most amazing opinions. But then,' he smiled sadly and reached out to touch my hand, 'you were an impressionable girl. You believed every word he said, even when he called your father a capitalistic blood-sucker. I'm afraid that was the phrase that started our final row. The very next day I heard you'd moved in here with David, broken off relations with your father ... So I decided to wash my hands of you.'

'I see,' I said faintly, holding my aching head.

'You made it up with your father, though, didn't you?' James asked. 'After you were married? It didn't go on like that?'

'Apparently it did,' I said. 'According to Marjorie, I haven't set foot in Butterford Hall since then. But ... whatever I may have thought about her then, she's very kind. I like her. As soon as she knew I was in trouble she came to me and insisted I should stay with them.'

'Maybe you see things differently now. How are you getting on with Bevy'

'Not very well, I'm afraid. He doesn't like me, understandably enough.'

'On the other hand,' James said with a frown, 'it would probably suit his purpose to keep the feud going. Bev always had his eye on

45

the main chance.'

I looked up, puzzled, unable to think straight. 'I'm not sure I follow you.'

His gesture encompassed the kitchen and the garden. 'You're not exactly living in the lap of luxury, are you? Yet your father was a wealthy man. What did he do—leave it all to your step-mother?'

'Yes, he did. But since I cut myself off from them . . .'

'Whatever you did,' James interrupted, 'it still isn't right. As I remember Mrs. Heyman, she wouldn't like to see you cut off without a penny. But whatever she feels is due to you, it will mean less for Bevis. I can't see him liking it, can you?'

I stared at the skin that was forming on my coffee, wrinkling in the slight breeze from the open door. James didn't know about the clause in my father's will which left half his money to me—if I made up the differences with my step-family. No, James couldn't know about that, but Bevis did. I hadn't thought of it before, but now it was all so obvious. Bevis was unfriendly because he didn't want me to form a relationship with his mother.

'He'd have had no look-in at all if your brother had lived,' James was saying. 'It's not right for him to lay claim to it all. Didn't you and David think of contesting the will?'

I looked at him, not answering. How could I answer when I didn't know?

'Although with the weird views your husband had,' James went on, 'he probably wouldn't have let you touch a penny. He didn't believe in security. Hand to mouth, day to day. Pam, what the hell did you ever see in him?'

'I wish you wouldn't keep asking me questions like that!' I leaped up from the table and went to lean in the doorway, the sunlight dazzling through the moisture in my eyes. 'I don't know! I can't even remember him. I'm nobody, from nowhere. I burst into life, fully grown, four days ago.'

'Don't, love.' His hands came on my shoulders, turning me round into his arms. 'I'm sorry. It's because I care about you. Finding you living like this ... It's not you. David Lane infected you, dragged you down. I suppose he was so different from every other man you'd met that he took you by storm, and with things as they were for you at home ... Don't cry, my love. Please don't cry. I'm here now. I'll take care of you.'

I pushed him away, dashing an impatient hand across my eyes. 'But I don't *know* you! Don't you understand? You're a complete stranger!'

He looked as though I had hit him. He turned away and stood with his head bent, saying unhappily, 'I'm sorry.'

'So am I,' I said hoarsely. 'Just give me time. I'm so confused. I'm lost in a world full of strangers. You keep telling me what I did, but

47

none of it's real. It doesn't seem to have any connection with me. Please try to understand.'

He looked round at me then, hope in his eyes. 'Will you at least let me see you? I'll start from scratch, if that's what you want. I'll try to forget that I've loved you for . . .' He stopped with his head cocked, listening. 'Is that a car?'

Then I heard it, too. It was nearly twelve thirty, my watch told me.

'It must be Bevis,' I said. 'James, please . . . don't say anything.'

'I'm not a complete fool,' he told me tightly. 'If you've got to stay at the Hall for a while the last thing I intend to do is antagonise your step-brother.'

Their voices came ahead of them. I heard the girl say something about, ' . . . picturesque, but horribly isolated. I don't know how she can live out in the wilds like this. Oh, look at that gorgeous clematis, Bev. Do you think she'll give me a cutting if I ask nicely?'

They came into the yard, pausing as they saw me. Lorraine was smallish, slim in a blue linen safari suit, with sun-streaked fair hair held back by a pair of sunglasses on top of her head. She looked at me curiously, taking in every detail of my appearance.

'Whose car is that?' Bevis demanded.

'Mine,' James said, stepping through the doorway. 'Hello, Bev. How are you?'

It was a moment before Bevis recognised him. He said, 'James? Good Lord,' and held

48

out his hand, though it was clear to me that he was less than delighted to see my visitor. 'When did you get back?'

'A couple of weeks ago.'

Bevis turned to the girl at his side. 'This is James Summerton, Lori. And my sister Pamela.'

Lorraine nodded at each of us, saying, 'Hello, hello,' and her eyes rested on me, still studying me.

'Well, I must be on my way,' James said. 'You ought to get Pam home, Bev. She hasn't been feeling too well. I'll see you soon, Pam.'

'Oh—yes. Goodbye, and thank you.'

He gave me a private smile and departed, leaving me alone with my step-brother and his girlfriend, who continued to scrutinise me closely.

'What did *he* want?' Bevis asked in a hard voice that managed to convey very clearly his low opinion of James.

'Nothing,' I replied. 'He only came to see me. He's allowed to, isn't he? An old friend . . .'

'If you say so.'

'Well . . . isn't he?' I asked uncertainly.

'Don't you remember?'

I had forgotten that he expected my return to the cottage to work convenient miracles. 'If I did, I'd be jumping for joy!' I said tartly. 'Can we please go now? I'll just clear up.'

I went back into the kitchen, tidying away

49

the coffee things. Bevis followed me and Lorraine stood in the doorway, watching me in a way I was beginning to find irritating.

'Doesn't this place seem familiar at all?' my step-brother wanted to know.

'No, it doesn't. I had hoped ... But no, it hasn't helped. If anything it's made things worse. Another hope gone. So you've lost your bet.'

He lifted a derisive eyebrow, saying nothing.

All at once I could no longer stand Lorraine's scrutiny. I turned on her impatiently. 'I'm not an exhibit in a zoo, you know. I have amnesia. It doesn't show, though. I haven't grown a tail, or come out in big blue spots. Just what are you staring at?'

Lorraine reddened, but answered calmly enough, 'You're not what I expected, that's all.'

'Oh really? Haven't you ever seen me before?'

'No, I haven't. But Bevis has told me a lot about you.'

'I'll bet he has,' I said grimly, glancing at my step-brother, who tightened his jaw and said tersely, 'Leave Lorraine alone.'

'Shall we go?' I suggested. How could I explain that my nerves were on edge, that the cottage gave me a creepy feeling, that all this was like some bad dream?

I relaxed on the back seat of the car, my eyes closed, feeling ashamed of my outburst to

Lorraine. If that was the sort of person I was then I didn't much like myself. It seemed that I spent most of my life doing stupid things. 'You were a fickle little thing,' James had said. 'An impressionable girl.' A butterfly, in other words, blown hither and thither by whichever wind blew strongest at the time. Flirting with Bevis, toying with James, captured finally by a man whose radical views had alienated me from my family.

And what, I wondered, had I felt like recently? Had I come to my senses and wished myself back in the kind of life my father had given me? And had I been too proud to approach Marjorie directly? Had I solved that dilemma by setting fire to my cottage? Oh, God! Questions, questions, and no answers. If only I could *remember*.

'Are you all right?' I heard Lorraine ask anxiously. 'She's crying, Bev.'

'I didn't know she could,' he said.

'Bev!'

'Well, what do you want me to do about it?'

'You could stop, or something.'

'It's all right,' I managed, wiping my eyes on my sleeve. 'I'm all right. It's just ... Lorraine, I'm sorry.'

She smiled at me over the back of the seat. 'Don't worry about it. I do understand. I'd be frightened out of my wits if it happened to me.'

It was wonderful to return to the safety of Butterford Hall and the gentle Marjorie, who said she could kick herself for letting me go to the cottage so soon. From now on I must rest and not try to force it.

Lorraine had lunch with us. The meal was tasty but I didn't have much appetite and afterwards excused myself to go to my room and lie down. I was exhausted by the events of the morning and wanted only to sleep, to stop thinking for a while.

It seemed that I lay awake for hours, my mind going around in circles. What James had said; Marjorie's version of the story; Bevis's antagonism . . .

I dreamed that I was back at the cottage, in the living-room as it had been before the fire. The scene was very clear, clothed in bright colours. The rug was orange, the curtains yellow, huge flowers painted around the fireplace. I was sitting on the couch. A hand-woven blanket covered it. And then there was a movement behind me. I turned in alarm, the picture growing grey. I cried out in terror. An indistinct form loomed over me, menacing, lunging for me . . .

I woke with a start, my body clammy with sweat. Even when I realised that I was safe in my room at Butterford Hall the fear held me in thrall. The dream had been so clear, so real. Like a memory.

A memory.

CHAPTER THREE

It was a long while before my pulse-beat returned to normal. I lay flat on my back, breathing deeply, letting every muscle in my body relax. A few hours ago I had almost decided that the most logical thing for me to do was to return to the cottage. That would show Bevis he was wrong about me and leave me free to do what I chose about that clause in my father's will—when I could remember what I thought about that. Perhaps it had always been my intention to remain independent.

But having spent two hours at the cottage and experienced the unease of the place, and now having dreamed of a murderous attack on me there, I did not face the prospect so happily.

It was, after all, only a dream, I told myself. There was no way of knowing what twists of thought were passing deep in my mind, what tortuous images my lost memory might be conjuring. I could not be entirely sure that my dream had pointed to the truth. But I felt it, just the same.

I decided to say nothing for the time being, but to let things ride and hope that the doctors were right when they told me that only by relaxing would my memory come back normally. They had supplied me with a bottle of tranquillisers which so far I had not taken regularly, though perhaps that was foolish. Perhaps I still needed chemical help.

Whether it was the drugs or partly because of my own acceptance of the situation, the few days that followed passed peacefully enough. I remained at Butterford Hall, for there seemed to be no reason for returning to the cottage. In that woodland environment the cats could easily fend for themselves for a while and I was happier drifting, not asking questions, merely letting life flow over me.

Marjorie approved of this state of affairs, though she did look out some photographs for me. They seemed like pictures from someone else's album, though, and I soon put them away.

Bevis was subdued during that time. Perhaps Marjorie had given him a lecture, but he didn't voice his doubts again in my hearing. In fact he barely spoke to me at all—being 'civil' as he had promised his mother.

In the middle of the week, Marjorie, Phyllis and I spent the morning in Cannonfield, where my step-mother insisted on buying me some clothes, more feminine than those which made up my original wardrobe. She wouldn't listen to my protests, but I inwardly vowed to pay her back as soon as possible.

'Now you look more like your old self,' she approved as I came down the stairs at Butterford Hall. 'I know these jeans and things are cheap, but you really needed a change or two. The only nice clothes you had were that blouse and suit you were wearing when they took you to hospital. I sent them to the cleaners, but there was blood on them and the jacket sleeve was burned. I don't know how they'll . . .' She broke off as the doorbell rang. 'Oh, excuse me, darling. Who on earth can that be?'

A young man wearing overalls stood on the doorstep, bearing a long florist's box and asking for Mrs. Lane. I accepted the box, thanking him, while Marjorie exclaimed in delight, wondering aloud who could be sending me flowers.

The box contained a dozen deep red long-stemmed roses, and a card which read, 'Just so you don't forget me again. See you at the weekend. James.'

'James?' Marjorie queried, reading over my shoulder. 'Oh—James Summerton. Bevis said he was back. He must be very keen. You . . . like him, do you?'

'You tell me,' I said ruefully. 'I've met him once, that I recall. You probably know him better than I do.'

'I vaguely remember him. One of the crowd. You were never short of young men, Pamela. But I know his aunt, Mrs. Ford. He's dark, isn't he? Rather good-looking'?'

'Yes, I'd say so.' Nice, too, I thought, looking at the lovely roses he had sent me. I could picture his face very clearly, that wry little smile and the brilliant blue eyes.

'You'd better put them in water,' Marjorie said. 'It's nearly lunchtime.'

*   *   *

When Bevis came home that evening the first things he noticed were the roses, which I had arranged in a vase in the sitting-room.

'Been treating yourself?' he asked his mother. 'Aren't there enough flowers in the garden?'

'Oh, those aren't mine,' Marjorie told him. 'They came for Pamela. From James Summerton.'

For some reason I immediately felt defensive. 'And why not?' I demanded as Bevis glanced enquiringly at me.

He shrugged. 'No reason on earth. But you *have* been shopping, I see. I'm glad you settled for something more feminine for a change. With that haircut, and always in jeans, you look more like a boy than a woman.'

'Do you have to practise, or does your charm come naturally?' I asked drily.

'Now, children.' Marjorie stood up and came between us. 'Don't squabble. Let's have dinner. Are you seeing Lorraine tonight, Bevis?'

'No, not tonight. It's your Guild meeting, isn't it? I thought I'd stay and keep Pamela company.'

'Oh, how nice!' she exclaimed. 'That's thoughtful of you, darling. Yes, the two of you can have a lovely chat together. Really get to know each other again.'

I was not so sure about Bevis's motives for his 'thoughtfulness'. Somehow the idea of an evening alone with him didn't strike me as idyllic. Once his mother was out of the way perhaps he would feel free to revile me again.

But the evening began quietly enough. I curled in the armchair where I usually sat, reading a novel, while Bevis put some music on the stereo-gram before settling opposite me with the new edition of *House and Garden*.

'Do you like this piece' he asked after a while. I stopped reading and gave my full attention to the piano playing softly. 'Yes, very much.'

'Do you know what it is?'

'Chopin. I don't know which one, though . . . How do I know it's Chopin?'

'It's not,' Bevis informed me. 'It's Liszt.'

'Oh.'

A small smile curved his mouth. 'I'm surprised you could even guess that close. Do you like classical music?'

'I . . .' I hesitated. 'Yes, I think so. Don't I?'

'I'm asking the questions.' He put down the magazine and fixed his eyes on my face. 'Who's your favourite composer? Don't think about it, just say a name.'

'Wagner,' I said at once.

'What especially?'

'Tannhäuser, I think.'

'The heroic stuff.'

'Yes.' I was amazed.

'Well, that's a start, anyway,' Bevis said with satisfaction. 'It's all still there, even if it's deeply buried. What else do you like?'

'In music?'

'In anything. Your favourite colour. TV programme. Do you prefer a play or a film?'

'Will that help?'

'It might. You'd be as well to try to remember generalities, not particulars. Something may just turn the key. At least you haven't lost your taste in clothes. Those frightful smocks and jeans must have been from necessity rather than choice.'

'I intend to pay your mother back as soon as I can,' I said stiffly.

Bevis dismissed that with a wave of his hand. 'That wasn't what I meant. Pamela ... I'm sorry for the way I behaved. If you'd been faking, you'd have tripped up by now. The feud wasn't any of my making, you know.'

'I realise that. I behaved abominably, didn't I? But I must have changed, Bevis.'

'Bev.'

'Sorry?'

'Everybody except mother calls me Bev. It's a stupid name, but I'm stuck with it.'

'Where did it come from?'

58

'Some book mother read just before I was born.'

'Oh, I see. I did wonder. Bevis Ennis is a bit of a . . .'

'Heyman,' he interrupted. 'Mother is only Mrs. Ennis because she married your father. Ennis was your maiden name. My surname is Heyman.'

'Yes, of course, I should have realised . . . I'm sorry. Bev Heyman.'

'Pam Ennis,' he returned with a sad little smile. 'A long time ago, wasn't it?'

'What was?'

'Nothing,' he said, and picked up his magazine.

For a moment I watched him thoughtfully. 'Did I hurt you very much?'

He slowly lifted his head until his eyes met mine. There was wariness in his expression. 'My pride, mostly. Who's been talking about that?'

'Does it matter, if it's true? I'll remember anyway, eventually. Don't you want to tell me?'

'I'd rather not.'

'Why?'

'Because I shall probably be extremely offensive and I'd rather not have a row tonight, if you don't mind.'

'Was I really so awful?'

'You were a bitch!' he said tersely, rattling the magazine as he turned his attention to an

59

article he was reading.

'Ten years ago?' I persisted. 'And you still haven't forgiven me? Isn't it possible I might have grown out of that phase by now?'

'That phase—and the rest,' he growled. 'All your phases have been unpleasant. Right now you aren't well. You're probably frightened by your amnesia. And, let's face it, you're taking tranquillisers. I don't doubt that once you get back to normal you'll be the same spoiled little brat you always were. Just a bit older, that's all.'

'Well, thank you,' I said faintly.

'I did say I'd rather not talk about it. I'm trying very hard to keep the peace—for mother's sake. But I'm not going to lie to you.'

'I don't want you to. Bev . . . I have changed. I'm appalled by some of the things I've been told about myself. That won't alter, even when I remember. Maybe living in that cottage, all alone, having to fend for myself . . . Couldn't it have made me turn over a new leaf?'

He looked up at me under his brows, saying doubtfully, 'Maybe.'

'Would you be happier if I went back to the cottage until we're sure?'

'Is that what you want to do?' he asked in surprise.

I hesitated, sighing, smoothing the open page of my book. I had no idea what had made me say that. 'I don't know.'

'Mother wouldn't stand for it, anyway,'

Bevis said. 'But I've been thinking we may as well make a start on cleaning the place up, if you feel up to it. There's no structural damage. A few floorboards, maybe, but I could do that. Lori's quite willing to help. Between the three of us we could make quite an impression on it over the week-end.'

'Four of us, perhaps. James is coming.'

'James!' he exclaimed with a laugh. 'I can't see him pitching in with us. He might get his hands dirty.'

'You don't like him, do you?' I said.

'It's mutual, I assure you. He and all the rest of your upper-crust followers never did think much to a 'pleb' like me being included in the social circle.'

'A "pleb"?'

'One of the lower classes. Your father had his own business and mixed with the gentry. *My* father worked with his hands. To your set, I was an upstart. That's what fascinated you— going around with the son of a labourer. Oh, I knew it. It amused me to see how uptight it made James Summerton and his crowd. In a way I was as bad as them.'

'I'm sure I never looked down on you,' I said.

'Oh, you did. You did. You were way up there on your pedestal and I was down in the mud. The novelty soon wore off. I knew you wouldn't take kindly to your father marrying my lowly mother, and how right I was. But

61

your father was no snob. He was the most genuine human being I've ever known.'

I was silent for a while, thinking. 'That's the third version I've heard—of my reasons for objecting to that marriage. Everyone sees it from a different angle. I wonder how *I* looked at it?'

'Sideways, with a scowl,' Bevis said flatly, but there was humour in his eyes and we both smiled at the absurdity of the way he had put it.

'You *have* changed,' he told me. 'The old Pam would have been spitting and scratching by now. I must say I prefer the new you.'

'You're nicer, too, when you're not being belligerent,' I said. 'Maybe there were faults on both sides.'

'Yes, you may be right.'

'And David didn't help much, did he?' I added. 'I gather he brain-washed me into his twisted way of thinking.'

Bevis frowned. 'The less said about David Lane the better. You couldn't seem to see that he was bent on destroying everything. He was bitter, malignant, communistic. He hated everybody because of some imagined wrong. I'm sorry to say it, but the world became just a little bit brighter with him out of it.'

'There must have been some good in him,' I said, 'I loved him, didn't I?'

'If you can call it love. You never talked to me about it. When anyone raised the subject

62

of David Lane you lashed out. I think in the beginning you were sorry for him. You appeared to see him as a victim of society. That's how he saw himself, of course. Once he'd got a hold of you, your mind wasn't your own. You even talked like him. But he made you miserable in the end.'

'Did he?' I was remembering the photograph at the cottage, the devil-may-care grin beneath the tousled hair.

'I brought mother to see you once,' Bevis said. 'It was soon after your father died. Mother wanted to make peace, but ... You were a mess. You had a black eye. You insisted that you had walked into a door, and then you turned nasty, mainly because we'd seen what sort of life you were living. Beer cans all over, everything untidy. You told us to stay away and stop interfering, so we did. We'd taken a lot from you, but that was the last straw. I only went to the cottage once more, after David was killed. Mother was concerned about you, so I went to see ... You wouldn't even open the door, Pamela. You shouted abuse at me. After that I stayed clear. We couldn't help you if you wouldn't let us.'

'I don't blame you for not wanting me here,' I said. Bevis surveyed me thoughtfully for a while, grey eyes studying my face. 'I keep expecting you to rear up and defend yourself. My view of things is probably jaundiced, you know.'

'It's the only view I have, at the moment. I can't take it personally. To me it's just a story, unconnected with me. I have to force myself to realise that ... Well, for instance, that the cottage is my responsibility. I haven't even bothered to find out about insurance. I ought to make a claim as soon as possible, don't you think?'

'You can have a look for the policy at the weekend. In the circumstances the insurance people will understand about the delay. I ought to have thought about it myself, but I didn't like to go poking around among your things.'

'And anyway you weren't going to put yourself out for my benefit,' I reminded him. 'It's nice of you to offer to help clean up, though. But won't it spoil your weekend?'

He gave me a small, sheepish smile. 'It was Lori's idea, if you must know. She likes you.'

'She's sorry for me,' I amended lightly. 'But I like her, too. How long have you know her?'

'About a year. She works in my office. Well, not exactly in the *same* office. She's secretary to one of the senior partners.'

'That's handy,' I said drily.

'Too handy, sometimes. Look ... I'm a bit concerned about your insurance, now that you've mentioned it. They might want someone to assess the damage before we start clearing up. Would you like to run over to the cottage now?'

'In the dark?' I said, horrified by the thought.

'You've got electric light, haven't you? It's not nine o'clock yet. We've plenty of time. We might as well be doing that as sitting here.'

'Well . . . yes, I suppose so. I'll get my coat.'

The valley was cloaked in darkness. A few lights showed from the houses in Butterford, but we were soon through the village and beginning the long climb out of the valley. When we turned off down the lane that led to my cottage the tunnel of branches looked eerie in the head-lights. There was a gusting wind that night, bringing down showers of leaves.

I climbed from the car, hearing the noise of the wind. Trees brushed against each other, invisible in the night, and the wind whipped my short hair about my head.

'I should have brought a torch,' Bevis said as we crunched our way down the path. 'Do you want me to go first?'

'No, I'm all right.' It was a lie. The night was alive with noise and I could hardly see a thing. Keeping a tight hold on my nerves, I let my feet follow the path, one hand out in front of me.

Something touched my face. I drew in my breath, alarmed.

'What's wrong?' Bevis asked anxiously, catching my arm.

'I walked into the hollyhocks,' I told him, furious with myself. Thankfully, I found the side wall of the cottage and let it guide me to the yard. I reached the door with no mishap but for the smashing of one of the cats' dishes, and let myself into the kitchen.

As I stood blinking against the bright light, Bevis closed the door, shutting out the sound of the tumult outside. The kitchen was as we had left it, but the sight of it, the gay colours in the room, brought my dream vividly back to me. I stared at the further door, unable to move towards it.

'Our best bet seems to be upstairs,' Bevis said, making for that door, opening it so that the acrid smell of the fire came strongly. 'Pamela?'

'I'm coming,' I said in a strangled voice. With my heart pounding loud in my ears I made myself go forward, but paused again on the threshold, remembering. That vague figure, lunging . . .

'Remember something?' Bevis asked.

Focusing my eyes, I saw the concern on his face. 'No. Nothing. Just a feeling.'

'That's not to be wondered at. But you're safe now. The fire's out. Here, take my hand . . . Grief, you're freezing! Come on, let's get into the hall.'

Switching on the light as he went, he led me down the hall, stopping by the front door to take two letters from the basket behind the letter-box.

'Your mail.'

'Thank you.' With trembling, hopeful hands, I opened the first envelope and took out a typed letter, and a cheque for fifty pounds. The letter was from someone named Patricia Hart, who said that the gingham mice were a great success and she would be glad to take another twenty. Her address was 'The Wishing Well, High Street, Cannonfield'.

'It's a shop,' Bevis said when I showed him the letter. 'Good glassware, chess sets, handmade stuff. Presumably you make gingham mice. Does it ring a bell?'

'No. But there are some bits of gingham in the work-room.'

'What's the other letter about?'

The second one was handwritten, asking me to telephone as soon as possible. The signature was almost illegible, but we guessed it was somebody Davies.

I looked hopefully at Bevis, but the name meant nothing to him.

'At least he's given you his number,' he said. 'Or she has. You can phone when we get home.'

'I can pay Marjorie for those clothes now,' I replied, putting the letters into my coat pocket.

Upstairs, he left me to search the main bedroom while he looked in the other two. It was like seeking the proverbial needle, hoping to find an insurance policy among all that disorder, but I tried, searching drawers and cupboards, even under the bed—though all I found there was a fat stuffed toy in the shape of a mouse, fashioned of pink gingham with eyes and whiskers embroidered in a cheeky expression, and huge floppy ears.

'Found anything?' Bevis asked, coming in with a shoe box in his hand.

'Only this.' I held up the fat mouse. 'Cute, isn't he?'

'Ghastly,' said Bevis. 'Look, I've come across some documents. Birth and marriage certificates, a letter about David's life insurance, which wasn't much. There's a little policy on your life, but it doesn't look as though it's been paid for months. I would have thought, if you had any house insurance it would have been here.'

I sat on the bed, looking at him forlornly. 'Then maybe I wasn't insured.'

'You never did have much of a head for money,' he said with a sigh. 'You're just lucky the damage wasn't worse.'

'Yes. I'm sorry, Bev. I've been pretty useless all round, haven't I?'

'You can't be decorative *and* useful,' he said ruefully 'You always had everything done for you. But you'll have to learn to cope, Pam.'

Sadly, sick of myself, I looked round the untidy room, my eyes falling on the picture of David. 'He doesn't really look like a maladjusted drop-out, does he?'

'Who?'

'David. That photograph.'

68

He picked it up, studied it, looked at me across it with one eyebrow crooked. 'That's not David.'

'Isn't it?' I asked, too numb to be much surprised. 'Then who . . . '

'I've no idea,' Bevis said, putting it carefully down. 'It's nobody I know. But *you* must know him. Maybe he'll turn up one of these days.'

'And add a few more pieces to the jig-saw. Oh Bev . . . I wish I could *remember!*'

'Hey, come on!' He caught my elbows, drew me to my feet. 'You're depressed. Let's go home. Bring Fred with you, if you like.'

'Fred?'

He nodded at the plump mouse I still had in my hands. 'Fred Mouse. You've got twenty more like him to make for The Wishing Well. We'll make a successful businesswoman of you yet.'

As we went down the stairs my fear returned, the fear of what had happened in that living-room. It was illogical, but so strong that I was more and more convinced that there had been something more than a simple accident. I gritted my teeth, trying not to show what I was feeling, and soon we were through that dark room whose light didn't work.

And then, as we went into the kitchen, a cat leapt onto the table. It appeared so suddenly that I cried out, my nerves jumping crazily.

'It must have come in when we did,' Bevis said, looking from the cat to my face. 'You *are* jumpy, aren't you? Better put it out, or it will make the place stink.'

'Shouldn't we feed it?'

'If you must.'

Opening another tin of catfood, I went out to scrape it into a dish that lay in the shaft of light from the kitchen. The cat failed to respond to the invitation. It remained on the table, tail lashing. Tentatively I reached out to take hold of it and it clawed at me, catching the back of my hand painfully. As I flinched away it shot off the table and out into the night.

'Bloody things!' Bevis said tersely. 'Did it hurt you?'

'It's nothing.' I put my hand under the cold tap, washing the three bleeding scratches. I wanted to burst into noisy tears, but I refused to let myself. Nothing was going right. Nothing.

Gently, Bevis wrapped a clean handkerchief round my hand. 'It's not your day, is it? I'm sorry our trip hasn't been more productive.'

'It's not your fault—it's mine. How could I have lived this way when all I had to do was swallow my pride and come . . . It's so damn stupid!'

'Yes, it is,' he agreed gravely. 'I'm glad you've finally seen that for yourself.'

He took my hand to guide me back down the path and I stayed close to him, glad of his presence that cold, blustery night. We didn't talk much until we were back in the warmth of Butterford Hall, when he helped me off with my coat and stood watching me thoughtfully.

'That cottage really gets on your nerves, doesn't it?'

'Yes.' An uncontrollable shudder ran through me. 'But you said yourself—that's only natural.'

He nodded silently, but I could tell from his expression that he was wondering if there was some other reason for my fear. I was on the verge of telling him about my dream when he turned away to put my coat in the hall cupboard and the moment passed. He would scoff, anyway. A dream was just a dream. In my right mind I would never have imagined it to be anything else.

'You'll want these,' he said, holding out the two envelopes from my coat pocket. 'Are you going to phone this Davies person? It sounded fairly urgent.'

'Oh . . . yes, I could try.'

He gestured at the phone. 'Help yourself. I'm going to pour us a drink. Give me a shout if you need me.'

I dialled the number, a local one, and stood listening to the purr-purr. Eventually a male voice answered, giving the number.

'Mr. Davies?' I asked. 'Good evening. This is Pamela Lane. I got your note.'

'Who did you say? Oh—Mrs. Lane? Wood End Cottage? How are you feeling now?'

'I'm much better thank you, but I'm afraid I don't know who you are. You see, I . . .'

'Your milkman,' he interrupted. 'Sorry, I should have said. Not many people know me by name. I expect you wondered what it was about. Well, you know last Wednesday—when you had that fire . . . I ought to have thought about it before but it didn't connect until I was talking to the wife about it yesterday and she said it was a bit strange. Nobody goes down to Wood End except to your cottage, apart from the young couples doing their courting, but that wasn't very likely on a day like that. So I wondered . . . there's a rumour going around that you don't remember what happened and I thought you might like to know. I mean, if I can help the police or anything . . .'

'The police?' I broke in.

'Aren't they investigating? Oh, well, I suppose not. I mean it was probably just an accident, a log falling off the fire or something and you tripping in your hurry. That's what I said to Sheila at the time. Lucky, you were. But then we were talking it over—you know how you do. First bit of excitement we've had in years—and I happened to mention this car that nearly put me in the ditch. That's when Sheila said it was funny, because if somebody had been at your cottage they'd have seen the fire, and if they weren't visiting you then what were they doing up the lane tearing along in such a flippin' hurry? We just thought it should be mentioned. I don't suppose there's anything in it, but you never know.'

'There was a car?' I repeated as he paused for breath. 'You mean ... just before you found me?'

'That's right. Coming right at me down the lane, it was, but I couldn't tell what make it was. The sky had just turned black—just before that storm—but I'd say it was a pale-coloured car. White, or maybe blue. It was only a couple of minutes after that that I saw the fire through your window. It had got a good hold. If I hadn't come just at that moment ...'

'I know,' I said. 'Mr. Davies, forgive me. I haven't thanked you. You saved my life, you know.'

'All in the line of duty, ducks. And if you want to express your gratitude, do me a favour and pay your bill. You owe me two pounds fifty-six up to that Wednesday. When do you want me to start delivering again?'

'I'm not sure.' My mind was in turmoil. A car? How odd. 'I'll let you know. And ... thank you again, Mr. Davies.'

'Don't mention it. Like I said—just pay the bill, will you? 'Bye.'

Leaning on the wall, I put down the phone. A dark, stormy morning, a car speeding away from the cottage where I lay unconscious with a fire creeping closer to me. Whose car?

A pale colour, he had said. White, or ...

73

Despite myself, my imagination showed me a clear picture of the car which even now stood on the drive of Butterford Hall. A Viva. A *white* Viva. Bevis's car.

CHAPTER FOUR

Alarmed, I glanced at the sitting-room door, but it was closed. Bevis couldn't have heard any of the conversation. Not that I believed he had anything to do with the fire. Of course I didn't believe it, I told myself angrily. Why should he want to harm me?

Why?—That damn will of my father's, that might be why. Bevis had accused me of deceit to gain half of that inheritance. Would he himself have done worse things, for all of that money?

No. No. That was leaping to conclusions. Bev had been nice to me recently, especially that evening. But why had he been nice? To allay suspicion? And why had he been so interested in my fear of the place? Was he afraid I might be beginning to remember?

It was frightening how doubts grew once they were allowed a tiny hold in one's mind.

As I opened the door, Bevis straightened from smelling my roses and I was aware of how powerful he was, tall and broad-shouldered.

'I poured you some brandy,' he said, indicating the glasses on the table. 'You looked as though you needed it. What was all that about?'

'Oh . . . Mr. Davies is the milkman—the one who rescued me, though he made very light of it.'

'And what did he want?'

I sank into a chair, taking a sip of the brandy, feeling its warmth spread down my throat. 'Just to ask when I wanted him to deliver again.'

'Was that urgent?' Bevis asked in surprise.

' It might have seemed so, to him. And he's a bit anxious because I haven't paid my milk bill. He's a very talkative man. I could hardly get a word in edgeways.'

'Oh, is that all?' He resumed his seat and changed the subject, so I breathed easily again. I had to think about what Mr. Davies had told me, get it into perspective before I mentioned it to anyone else. That mysterious car might have nothing to do with me at all.

*   *   *

However, I soon had other things to worry about. The following afternoon I was cleaning my room when Phyllis Franklin rushed in, very disturbed, saying something about Marjorie and a man. I switched off the vacuum cleaner so that I could hear her properly.

'... and he's really being awfully rude to her. I think you ought to come. After all, it's not Marjorie's fault.'

'What isn't?' I asked, perplexed. 'Who do you say this man is?'.

'Your landlord!' Phyllis cried. 'He's threatening her with a solicitor.'

I ran down the stairs and into the sitting-room, where a large, bald-headed man in a black overcoat was talking forcefully to my step-mother. He paused as I went in, turning bulbous dark eyes on me.

'Ah—Mrs. Lane. There you are.'

'She's not well, I tell you,' Marjorie protested. ' Surely this can wait?'

'I'm afraid not. I've given her more than a reasonable amount of time. Mrs. Lane, I've been to my cottage. You'll have to put it right before you leave, of course. It's entirely your responsibility. You should have had the fire guarded. I want it done as soon as possible, please. You'll be hearing from my solicitor. I'll give you a month. That's more than you deserve, but I want to be fair. A month, and then—out!'

I stared at him blankly, trying to assimilate this new information. 'Out? You mean ...'

'I mean I want my property back. That's plain enough, surely?'

'But ... but ... I thought the cottage was mine!'

'Yours!' he roared.

Marjorie stepped in, diminutive beside his black bulk. 'I've been trying to explain to you, Mr. Curtis. My daughter has amnesia as a result of the fall she had. She doesn't remember a thing. I, too, was under the impression that the cottage had belonged to her husband.'

'Well, it didn't,' he said, glowering. 'It belongs to me. And this is the fourth consecutive month she hasn't paid her rent. I've been patient. I've been reasonable. I know she's lost her husband and is having a difficult time of it, but there are limits. I rely on that rent for additional income. I've got five teenage children to feed and clothe. If she can't pay her rent then I'll find a tenant who can.'

'How much does the rent come to?' Margorie asked.

'One hundred and thirty-six pounds, plus damages if she can't get that seen to. That's to date, to the end of this week.'

Stunned, I sank in to a chair. I heard Marjorie say pertly, 'Will you take a cheque?'

'Marjorie, no!' the gasp was torn from me. 'I can't let you . . .'

'We'll call it a loan,' she said, reaching for her hand-bag.

After considerable argument, I countersigned my fifty pound cheque from the Wishing Well and gave it to Marjorie, who then wrote out a cheque for the full amount of the rest. The sight of the figures seemed to appease Mr. Curtis.

'But if it happens again,' he said, 'I'll have to take action sooner. I'm sorry about this, particularly as you're Frank Ennis's daughter. I knew him quite well. I respected him. To see his daughter running up debts here there and everywhere ... He'd turn in his grave if he knew.'

'There's no call to exaggerate,' Marjorie said tightly. 'She may have got behind with the rent, but ...'

'Not only the rent. Word has been going round. She owes money at the village shop, and the garage that put new tyres on her bike. I'm sorry, Mrs. Ennis, but you've a right to know. There's not a person left in Butterford that would give her credit. Good afternoon.'

*　　*　　*

I wandered disconsolately up through the woods behind Butterford Hall and came to a stile, beyond which a path led down into the next valley. There were no trees there, only the open moors, craggy with rocky outcrops and coarse, sheep-nibbled grass. The path was steep, ending at a plank bridge across the stream that rippled clear over rounded stones, and beside the stream there was a granite ledge which provided a natural seat for my weary bones. From that angle I might have

78

been the only human being for miles around.

High in the cloudy sky a lark sank plaintively as if mourning the passing of summer. There was an autumnal chill in the air, but my seat was shaded from the stiff breeze which had followed the gales of the previous night. l forgot about time as I vainly tried to see some way out of the mess my life had become.

I leaned against a shoulder of rock, the light wind caressing my face. It was so peaceful there that I became drowsy and my mind slipped its moorings and went roaming. A picture began to build in my head. I fancied I heard a seagull cry, and the sound of the sea. I was perched on a clifftop with waves glinting far below me. To my left lay a small village with a harbour where boats bobbed at anchor. And then there came footsteps behind me, someone I knew, someone for whom I was waiting. His name . . .

'Pam?'

Startled, I jerked fully awake, the image dispersing with a jolt. Bevis stood beside me, wearing a thick-knit sweater and grey slacks.

'I thought you were someone else,' I said.

'Oh? Who?'

Closing my eyes, I tried to remember the name of that other man, but it had gone again. 'I don't know. Someone I used to know. I almost remembered something—a fishing village, and a cliff.'

'Remembered?' Bevis queried. 'Or dreamed?'

'I'm not sure.' My mind was back in the present, recalling all too clearly the events of the past few days. Bevis didn't seem angry, so perhaps Marjorie hadn't told him about our visit from Mr. Curtis. 'Are you home from work? Is it that late?'

'Just after five. I left the office early. I went to that shop—The Wishing Well—to let them know the situation. Patricia Hart says there's no rush for the mice.'

'Oh, I see. Thank you, that was thoughtful, Bev. At the moment I wouldn't know where to begin . . .'

'There's another thing,' he broke in, putting one foot on the ledge beside me and leaning on his knee, looking down at his shoe. 'Mrs. Hart's husband came in while I was there and she was telling him what had happened to you. When I left he came after me and asked again how you were, if you were really all right. And he asked how it happened, whether it was an accident. He seemed unusually concerned, but when I commented on it he said it was just polite interest.'

Watching his serious face, I felt my heart contract with alarm. 'What else could it have been?'

'That's what bothers me, Pam.' His eyes met mine, grey as the cloud moving behind him. 'His wife called him Alan. Alan Hart. Does

80

that mean anything to you?'

'Not a thing. Should it? Do you think he knows me?'

'I think you know each other, pretty well. Why else would you have a photograph of him in your bedroom?'

*   *   *

I had known he had something unpleasant to tell me, but this! Another woman's husband . . .

'O, God!' I stood up, wrapping my arms about myself. 'I can't stand much more of this. No wonder I can't remember. I must have just switched it all off because I couldn't bear it. Bev . . . you may as well know now as later. My landlord came today. I owe him over a hundred pounds.'

'Landlord?' he repeated in astonishment.

'His name is Curtis. Bev . . . your mother paid him. I gave her that cheque for fifty pounds, but it was more than twice as much. I owe money all over the place. The milkman, the village shop, the garage . . . And now you tell me I'm involved with a married man! What else is there that my mind refuses to acknowledge? What else have I done?'

He stared at me silently, thoughts racing behind his eyes, frightening me.

'Bev! What are you thinking?'

'Nothing,' he said roughly, catching my arm.

'Come on, let's go back. It's dinnertime.'

Somehow I managed to change my clothes, wash my face, brush my hair, though I did it automatically, my mind elsewhere. Life had to go on, I told myself. Take each moment as it comes. Don't think about the past, or the future.

But I did spare a moment to close my eyes and relive the scene on the cliff, sure now that it had been a memory. I knew that coastal village, had been there often. But the whole reality of it eluded me each time I tried too hard to grasp it. It left me with an aching sense of loss.

Going down to dinner, I heard Bevis talking in a low, insistent voice, but he stopped as I went into the dining-room. Marjorie glanced at me nervously, something between sorrow and fear in her eyes. I guessed that they had been discussing the money paid to Mr. Curtis.

'I'll pay her back,' I said in a low voice, addressing Bevis. 'I swear I'll pay back every penny, if I have to scrub floors to do it.'

'Darling!' Marjorie said brokenly. 'There's no need . . .'

'There's every need,' Bevis broke in. 'Pam has to work this out for herself. We'll help—of course we will—but it's up to her to decide what she does. It's time she faced up to things squarely. She's tough enough to do it if we let her. Aren't you, Pam?'

Perplexed, I shook my head. 'Do you think

so?'

'You've got to be,' my step-brother told me. 'Turning over a new leaf, remember? There's really no alternative, is there?'

'No,' I said. 'No, I suppose not.'

'But this time you won't be alone,' Marjorie said softly, a catch in her voice. 'You'll never be alone again, Pamela.'

As had so often happened lately I had no appetite, but with Marjorie's worried eyes upon me I forced down small helpings.

'You don't eat enough to keep a sparrow alive,' my step-mother commented. 'No wonder you're so thin. You used to be such a fine, healthy girl.'

'I'm just not very hungry,' I said. 'Marjorie . . . did the doctor say how long this amnesia would last?'

Her eyes slid away from me. She said evasively, 'Didn't he tell you?'

'He only said I should take it easy, and be patient. But surely there's some pattern in these cases?' I looked to Bevis for help, but he only gazed at me unhappily.

'Well—isn't there?' I persisted. 'For heaven's sake, tell me!'

'It all depends,' Bevis said quietly.

'On what?'

'That, I don't know. There are several things that might happen. Your memory may come back all at once, or bit by bit—though it's probable you'll never remember clearly the few minutes just before you blacked out.' His tone of voice told me there was more.

'Or?' I prompted.

He pushed his plate away, folding his hands in front of him. ' Or you may never remember at all. It does happen, apparently. It's something you must be prepared for.'

'But it needn't make any difference,' Marjorie encouraged. 'The whole future lies before you. Unhappy memories would only spoil your life. Perhaps you're lucky to be able to start afresh.'

Lucky! Lucky to have lost nearly twenty-eight years of my life? I couldn't see it that way at first. Needing solitude, I spent the evening in my room, slowly coming to terms with the possibility of never remembering anything before my waking in the hospital.

Three times Marjorie came to 'make sure you're all right, darling', and when I was on the verge of sleep I was again aware of her looking in to check on me. Was she worried that I might go to pieces now that I knew the worst?

My step-mother's concern was still noticeable the following day. We went shopping at a nearby supermarket and when we returned to the Hall I helped Phyllis make lunch, but Marjorie was never far away and kept coming in to smile and ask, 'All right?'

During the afternoon I decided to go for a walk only to have Marjorie insist on coming along, saying that she herself could do with some air. I looked at her standing there with her windblown hair, gardening gloves and trowel.

'Aren't you getting enough air in the garden?' I asked amusedly. ' I shan't get lost, you know.'

'No, I'm sure you won't, but ... I could do with a walk.' She was too honest to be good at lying. Not half an hour before she had said that her legs were aching with rheumatics.

'If you're so determined to keep me company,' I said, 'why don't I come and help you in the garden? Though you'll have to show me what to do.'

Her face flooded with pleasure, and not a little relief. 'That would be lovely. There's so much to be done at this time of year.'

Albert Franklin was busy sweeping up leaves from the wide, sloping lawns preparatory to giving the grass its last cut of the year. Despite his constant efforts the garden was much too big for one man to keep entirely neat and Marjorie enjoyed pottering about among the flowers. She showed me how to prune the roses and spray them with fungicide, while she took cuttings from her prized herb garden. Although it was a cool day, the sun shining intermittently between swathes of cloud, it was pleasant to be outside in warm clothing.

Having finished her task she came to stand by me. 'We'll make a gardener of you yet.

85

Oh—listen to me. I'd forgotten that vegetable patch at the cottage. I must say I was surprised how well you were getting along with it, but I suppose it's partly the artist in you. You were always very artistic. You ought to bring your paints and things from the cottage. It would be good therapy. You may have lost your memory, but I bet you've still got your talent.'

I looked doubtfully at my hands. ' Do you think so? All the same, it's hard to earn money with that sort of thing. What did I do before I was married?'

'Do? In what way?'

'What job did I have?'

'You tried several different things, but none of them suited you. Anyway, you didn't need to earn money. Your father supported you.'

I sighed heavily. That was the sort of thing I was becoming used to hearing. 'You mean I was a parasite,' I said heavily.

'Oh no! Your father didn't mind.'

'But I ought to have minded. If I was so proud . . .' I shook myself. What I felt now was what mattered. 'All that's over. I've decided what I intend to do now, with your approval.'

Marjorie regarded me worriedly. 'There's really no hurry. It's only a week since . . .'

'The time isn't important. I'm well enough to work. I've been thinking about it all day, and most of last night. To begin with, may I come and live here? I'll pay you for my keep, of course.'

'Oh, but . . .'

'Please, Marjorie! Let me tell you all of it. I know I've no right to expect your help after the way I've behaved towards you, but I'm going to need help if I'm ever to get straight. The cottage is an unnecessary extravagance at the moment, and anyway . . . I don't think I could ever live there again. I'll give it up and come here, if you and Bevis agree, and then I'll get a job and pay off my debts. Once that's all settled I can think again. It seems to me to be the best way of doing it—solving the present problems before deciding what comes next.'

'That's very sensible,' she approved. 'Of course you can stay here. I keep telling you—it's your home. And I won't hear another word about paying for your keep. That's nonsense. I've always felt very bad about the way we seem to have . . . what's the word?—'disinherited' you. If your father hadn't married me, this house and everything would have been yours.'

'And if I hadn't been such a foul-tempered bitch,' I added. 'Anyway, that's my plan of campaign. It only remains to see what Bevis thinks about it.'

'He'll be as pleased as I am,' she assured me. 'All that unpleasantness last weekend . . . He was angry on my behalf, you know. He was just sticking up for me. Now he realises I don't need defending because you're not really the ogre we'd imagined you to be. As a matter of fact, he said only last night that it would be as well if you stayed here. We don't want you getting in that state again. We'd never forgive ourselves if . . .' She bit her lip, looking guilty, as if she had said more than she should, then swiftly reached up to kiss my cheek. 'But everything's all right now, isn't it?'

'Yes, everything's fine,' I said, but I wondered what it was that she had stopped herself from saying.

Dirty from the garden, I decided to have a bath and wash my hair before dinner. I gave myself the luxury of a long soak in the hot water, but twice Marjorie tapped on the door to check that I was 'all right'.

I borrowed her hairdryer and was sitting in my underwear tending to my hair when Phyllis came in bringing the suit and blouse I had been wearing on the day of the accident. The laundry van had just made its weekly visit to the Hall.

'They've made an effort to repair the sleeve,' she said as she hung the garments on the outside of the wardrobe. 'But it's never going to look the same. Pity. It's an expensive suit, from the looks of it. You would have to be wearing your best outfit.'

'It can't be helped,' I said.

'No, I suppose not. You all right, are you?'

'I'm fine! Don't I look fine? Why does everybody keep asking me? Marjorie's been like an anxious mother hen all day.'

'That's not to be wondered at,' Phyllis said darkly.

'Isn't it?' Perplexed, I glanced in the mirror. There was more colour in my cheeks than had been there all week. My eyes were bright and clear. Now that the plaster was off and my hair clean, covering the place, I looked perfectly healthy.

'Bevis had no right to go worrying her with his theories,' Phyllis said. 'I mean, now that you're here, looked after, you're not likely to do it again, are you? No, of course not. I keep telling her so, but she does like to worry.'

I turned to look it her. ' Not likely to do what, Phyllis? What has Bevis been saying?'

'Marjorie said I wasn't to tell you.'

'But you will, won't you'?'

'Well, if you're twisting my arm ... Bevis thinks you tried to kill yourself. He says you'd got yourself into such a hole that suicide must have seemed the only way out. But you're not suicidal now, are you? Only for goodness' sake don't tell Marjorie I told you. She told me in confidence. She always tells me everything, you know.'

Poor Marjorie, I thought. That was twice in a week that Phyllis had let her tongue run away with her. I wondered who else she talked to about the family's private matters.

Bevis had telephoned to say he would be dining with a client that evening, so Marjorie and I had dinner alone together. I took care to tell her how much better I felt now that I had come to a decision about the future. I intended to live on the assumption that my memory would never come back. Since I now knew that my past was not very savoury the thought didn't worry me too much.

'I'm sure I remembered something yesterday, though,' I said as we attended to the washing up. 'I can see it now—a village on the coast, near some cliffs. It was a happy memory.'

'A holiday?' Marjorie suggested. 'Your honeymoon, perhaps?'

'Maybe so. I wasn't alone, anyway. There was a man ... but that's where it gets hazy. Was it David, I wonder? ... No, it won't come any clearer.'

'Where's your ring?' Marjorie asked suddenly. 'Your wedding-ring? Oh Pamela ... That just shows how much weight you've lost, for it to drop off.'

I looked blankly at my naked left hand, trying vainly to remember when I had last been aware of the ring.

We searched the kitchen floor, to no avail; then I went upstairs to look in my bedroom while Marjorie checked the dining-room. The ring was nowhere to be seen.

I was on my knees in the bathroom when Marjorie called up the stairs to me.

'Have you found it?' I shouted back.

'No. Leave it for now. You've got a visitor.'

It was James Summerton, carrying a bouquet of yellow chrysanthemums. I paused on the stairs, my heart thumping, wishing he wouldn't smile at me that way when I hardly knew him. Marjorie had tactfully disappeared.

'Have I come at a bad moment?' he asked.

'No, not really. We were looking for my ring. I can't think where I've lost it.' I reached the hall and stopped self-consciously. 'Thank you for the roses.'

'It was my pleasure. These are for you, too. Do you like flowers?'

'Very much. Thank you.' I took the bouquet. The blooms were large and heavy. I couldn't think what to say to him.

He put one finger beneath my chin, making me look at him. 'Aren't you pleased to see me?'

'Yes, of course.'

'And how are you now? You look marvellous.'

'Oh, I'm fine, thank you.'

'But you still don't remember? Not anything?'

'Nothing. I'm sorry ... please come in the sitting-room. This way ... Oh, Marjorie, this is James Summerton.'

'So he told me,' she said with a shy smile. 'And of course I remember him now. Sit down, James. Let me take the flowers, Pamela.' She relieved me of them, smiling at them. 'Aren't they gorgeous? Now you talk to James. I've got things to do. Give him a drink if he wants one. Just make yourselves at home.'

As she left the room James stood by the settee, but I ignored the unspoken invitation and sat down in my usual chair.

'Well,' he said with one of his wry little smiles, 'at least your step-mother is glad to see me. Oh—it's all right, love. I know you don't mean to be frosty.' He perched on the arm of the settee, looking round the room appreciatively. 'I'd forgotten how nice this house is. I'd have been here sooner, only I'm working in Sheffield at the moment so it's a bit far during the week. I've foisted myself on my aunt for the weekend again.'

'Don't you have any other relatives?' I asked.

'Parents, and an older brother. The country seat's in Cumbria. I don't get up there very often. What happened to your hand?'

'What?' I glanced down at my right hand, where the three long scratch marks stood out clearly. As I recounted what had happened, James came to take my hand, kneeling beside me.

'You should take better care of yourself,' he said, gently kissing the scratches one by one before looking up at me with those deep blue eyes full of affection. 'I can't help it, Pam. I've got to touch you. Can I just sit here and hold your hand? Tell me what you've been doing all this week.'

'Being very lazy. And James ... I've discovered a lot of things about myself that you probably won't like. I've run up debts all over the place, and in my bedroom at the cottage there's a photograph of a man who, it turns out, is married to someone else. I may not be the kind of girl you think I am.'

'Oh, rot! You're human. I don't expect a saint.'

He asked questions and I found myself pouring out the whole story, even down to the letters we had found at the cottage. It was easy talking to James, who sat by my feet holding my hand and watching me with concern and sympathy.

'And did you call this man Davies?' he asked. 'Who is he? What did he want?'

'He's my milkman. I hadn't paid that bill, either. But ...' Hesitating, I decided it was time to share my doubts with someone. 'He saw a car driving at speed away from the cottage, just before he found me.'

'A car?' His eyes widened. 'What sort of car? Who was driving?'

'He couldn't see. It was blowing up for a storm, apparently, and you know what that lane's like with all those trees ... He could only tell it was a white car, or perhaps blue. James, I haven't told anyone else. I wasn't sure what to do. It needn't have any bearing on anything, need it?'

'Maybe not, but it seems damn peculiar to

me. There's nothing down there except that cottage. And why was he in such a hurry?'

'But if we assume he was leaving the cottage, that means . . .'

'It means that what happened to you was no accident,' James said grimly. 'Which leaves us with the next question—who would want to . . . My God, Pam, Bevis's car is white. I saw it last Sunday.'

'Yes.' I hung my head miserably. 'I know. But surely he wouldn't . . .'

'Why wouldn't he? Pam, I'm sorry to ask this, but what was in your father's will? Did he leave all his money to Bev's mother, or was there more than that?'

'There was a proviso. But it still doesn't mean that Bevis . . .'

'Tell me!' James insisted.

I looked down at his tanned face. It was unfair of him to demand an answer. 'I can't, James. It's private.'

'But was there some clause that might have benefited you?'

'Yes, there was. I'll say no more than that.'

'So Bev might have had reason for wanting you out of the way?'

'He might. But he didn't. He's been very nice to me these past few days.'

'Or does he feel safe because you can't remember what happened? You must be on your guard. Suppose you do suddenly remember.'

94

'I may not. The longer it goes on, the more I think I shall never know. But I did have an odd dream after my first trip to the cottage. I saw that room as it used to be, and then someone—it was just a shape, a shadow—it attacked me, and I woke up.'

Still holding my hand tightly, James regarded me with worried blue eyes. ' I don't like any of this. You ought to tell the police about it.'

'Tell them what? It's accepted that what happened to me was an accident. And I can't say what happened. It's all hints and disconnected bits and pieces that can probably be explained quite innocently.'

'And suppose they can't?'

'I just refuse to believe that Bevis . . .'

'Who else is there?' James demanded. 'As far as I can see, he's the only one with motive enough.'

'As far as we can see,' I repeated flatly. 'That isn't very far, is it? If I could remember, there might be half a dozen people with reason for killing me.'

'Don't be ridiculous! Nobody has that many enemies. But all right, we won't jump to any conclusions. We'll call him Mr. X. He has tried once to kill you.'

'But . . .'

'Just for the sake of argument, allow me to make the point . . . Having tried, and failed, the chances are he will try again.'

I could only stare at him, horror-stricken.

'He's safe at the moment,' James went on, 'but he can't be sure he'll stay safe. Any day now, your memory may come back. I don't want to frighten you, love, but you must take care. It's too big a risk to ignore.'

CHAPTER FIVE

There was a stillness within me, horror and panic waiting to erupt. Then abruptly it died, mainly because I didn't choose to believe what James had said. I couldn't have lived with the thought of danger lurking behind every moment. I'd have gone mad. It was supposition, that was all, ifs and buts, with a maybe or two thrown in, and probably entirely wrong.

'We're making a mountain out of a molehill,' I said with a sigh. 'Things like that don't happen to ordinary people.'

'The world is full of ordinary people, and "things like that" happen every day, somewhere.'

'It's more likely that I tried to kill myself, James. I'd thought of that even before Bevis did. I must have been in a terrible state.'

'Bevis told you he thought that . . .'

'No. He told Marjorie it might be the answer.'

James frowned and stood up, leaning on the stone chimney breast. 'If you ask me, Bevis is having a hell of a lot too much to say on the subject. Why does he suddenly think it has to be more than an accident? Is he afraid other people are beginning to wonder? Why does he know more about it than anyone else? He hadn't seen you for ages, had he?'

'Not since ... soon after David was killed, he said. But he's naturally concerned, James. For me, and for his mother.'

'And for your father's money,' James said grimly. 'Perhaps you don't realise just how much that is. There was the business, and his shares, not to mention this house. Your father was one of the wealthiest ...'

He stopped abruptly as Marjorie came in, beaming, bearing the chrysanthemums in a vase.

'They really are gorgeous,' she enthused. 'Excuse me, James, I'll put them here in the hearth. There! They brighten up that dark fireplace beautifully ... I've looked everywhere for your ring, Pamela, but I can't find it. You must have dropped it when we were gardening. We'll have a search out there tomorrow.'

'It really isn't important,' I said.

'Of course it is! Your wedding ring ...'

'A wedding, and a husband, that I don't even remember.'

Marjorie looked sad for a moment, then

brightened and smiled at us both. 'I've made some coffee. I thought you might like some. Do you mind if I join you now? I don't want to interrupt if you're talking privately.'

We both assured her we were doing nothing of the kind.

The conversation revolved mainly around James' Aunt Harriet, who sounded to be a lovable eccentric. A maiden lady, she lived alone in a big house near Cannonfield, belonged to the Women's Guild and various other associations, grew orchids, and collected hats. From descriptions by both James and Marjorie, I gathered a hilarious picture of Aunt Harriet in feathers, flowers, tulle and straw.

We were all laughing when Bevis walked in. He looked tired and it was plain he wasn't pleased to find James there. For a moment, as the two men stared at each other, I was afraid that harsh words were about to be exchanged, but Marjorie rose and began pouring drinks, asking Bevis if his business had gone well, and the moment passed.

'James, what will you have?' Marjorie asked, poised by the drinks cupboard.

'Nothing, thanks.' He got languidly to his feet. 'I must be going. I told Aunt Harriet I wouldn't be late.'

'Are you joining us tomorrow?' Bevis enquired.

'Tomorrow?' James glanced questioningly

at me. 'What's happening tomorrow?'

Without giving me time to open my mouth, my step-brother replied, 'We're making a start on repairs at the cottage.'

'You're going to do it yourselves?' James sounded astonished by the very idea.

'We thought we would,' Bevis said, a mocking light in his eyes. 'It's not beyond our capabilities. A few floor-boards, a lick of paint ... Are you any good with a scrubbing brush?'

'I might surprise you,' James replied. 'Yes, I'll be there. See you tomorrow, then. Goodnight, Mrs. Ennis. Thank you for the coffee.'

I followed him to the front door to see him out. In the hall he took my hand and held it to his chest, gazing at me with earnest blue eyes.

'Were you seriously planning to be alone at your cottage with Bev?'

'Alone?' I repeated. 'No, Lorraine is coming, too. But even if she wasn't ... James, I won't believe that Bev would hurt me. I can't believe it. Just because you don't like him ...'

'It's not only that,' he denied. 'It's logic. Someone tried to kill you, Pam. I know it's not a pleasant thing to live with, but it's the only reasonable answer. You're not the suicidal type, and I don't believe you got that lump on your head by accident. Someone left you unconscious, to die in that fire. For God's sake be careful—of everyone.'

My hand locked tightly round his, I stared at him, frightened by the assurance in his voice. He had no doubts. He was sure there had been an attempted murder. The trouble was, I was beginning to believe it, too.

'Don't look like that, darling,' he said anxiously, his free arm curling about my waist. 'I only want to impress on you the importance of being on your guard. Don't go wandering in lonely places. That's all.'

That's all! To know that someone—someone unknown, for when I thought of Bevis it seemed impossible to imagine him as a murderer—had tried to kill me. But in Marjorie's tender care I need have no fear of being alone, so that unknown someone would have no opportunity to try again.

Bolstered by these optimistic thoughts, I told James not to worry, let him kiss me, and saw him out of the house, though as I closed the door the niggling thought was back in my mind. Who hated me so much? And why? There was one other person I had been close to, of course—Alan Hart, who had a wife. Could that have any connection with what had happened to me?

'What a charming young man,' Marjorie remarked as I returned to the sitting-room. 'He's obviously very fond of you, Pamela. Is it mutual?'

'I like him,' I said. 'But I hardly know him, do I?'

Marjorie sighed. 'Of course. I was forgetting. You don't remember having known him before.'

'Or why she finished with him,' Bevis put in darkly.

Amazed by this obtuse comment, I asked him what he meant and he said, 'Nothing.'

'Then why say it?' Marjorie wanted to know. 'Bevis, if you know something . . .'

'I don't,' he said with a shrug. 'It's only what I surmised at the time, but I could be wrong. I never did like James Summerton much.'

'Why not?' his mother demanded.

Irritably, Bevis rose from his chair and went to refill his glass. 'Why should I? Grief, mother, nobody can like everybody else in the world—except you, perhaps. You only see the good in people. Anyway, Pamela likes him; you think he's wonderful . . . surely one of us is allowed a little antipathy?'

'I would have thought you'd had enough of that,' Marjorie said with a significant glance at the glass of whisky in her son's hand. 'Or are you just tired? You've been in a funny mood ever since you came in. Is anything wrong?'

'Nothing at all,' Bevis said in a tone that told her to mind her own business.

For a moment Marjorie watched him, obviously worried, then she rose stiffly from her chair. 'Well, I'm tired if you're not. I think I'll go to bed and rest my legs. They've been killing me all day. We must be due for some rain.'

When she had gone the room was very quiet. I sat looking at the bright chrysanthemums etched sharply against the blackness of the empty grate, aware of Bevis standing silently some feet away beyond my right shoulder. Although I couldn't see him, his face was clear in my mind, dimming the view of the flowers in the hearth. The fair hair with its tendency to curl, eyes of a clear grey deep-set, the firm chin and mouth . . . the face of a murderer? No, it was unbelievable.

'You're a proper little chatterbox tonight,' he said drily. 'What are you thinking about?'

'What did you mean about James and me?' I asked without turning. 'If you know something that I ought to know . . .'

'I know nothing! How can I, when I wasn't there? As I think I said before, my point of view may be distorted. Anyway, hasn't James told you about it?'

'He said we quarrelled, over the opinions I picked up from David.'

'Then maybe that's what happened. Why are you questioning it? Don't you trust him?'

I turned in my chair, my arm along the back, so that I could see him. 'Why won't you give me a straight answer, Bev?'

'Is my opinion so important?' he asked with a frown. 'It was a long time ago, Pam. It's not up to me to interfere in your private life.

102

You're capable of making your own decisions about James, as he is now, without me clouding the issue.'

'Considering your dislike of him,' I commented, 'you're being very fair-minded all of a sudden.'

One corner of his mouth curved up. 'Believe me, it's not easy . . . Mother tells me you've decided to give up the cottage and stay here.'

I was aware that he had deliberately changed the subject, but I went along with it. 'Yes. Do you mind?'

'Should I?'

'Well . . . you might.'

'Why?'

'You know why!' I exclaimed. 'After the way I've behaved . . . the black sheep begging entry back to the fold—your fold.'

'Yours, too. You weren't kicked out, you know. You left of your own free will. I've no right to bar the door, even if I wanted to. It's mother's house.'

'All the same, it would be easier with your approval. I'll work, Bev. I'll get a job and pay your mother back.'

In silence, he moved to the settee and sat down, watching me with a puzzled air. 'You really are anxious to put things right, aren't you? All right, if you want my approval you have it. You're welcome. If nothing else it will make mother happy.'

'Thank you.'

'You have changed,' he commented.

'Maybe I've grown up at long last.'

'Did you tell James about . . . about the mess you were in?'

'I thought it was only fair that he should know. Yes, I told him about the debts and about . . . that man, Alan Hart.'

Bevis looked shocked. 'You didn't give James his name, I hope?'

'No, of course I didn't. But Bev . . . when you went to the shop that day—to The Wishing Well—did you see Alan Hart's car?'

'Car? Why?'

'Never mind why! Did you see it? Did he arrive in a car?'

'Yes, he did. Parked it so close to mine that he had to move his to let me out. And I'll say it again—why?'

'What colour was it?'

His brows contracted with puzzlement. 'What difference does it make? Have you remembered something?'

'Please. Just tell me.'

'It was grey—No, I tell a lie, it was beige, a sort of dirty biscuit colour. A battered-looking thing.'

'Beige,' I said fatly. 'Would you call that a pale colour?'

'Yes, I suppose so. And now will you please tell me what all this is about?'

I hesitated, knowing I had been clumsy. It had not been my intention to arouse his

104

suspicions, but now that it had happened my instinct told me to be frank. I wanted to see his reactions.

'You remember that note I had from Alfred Davies?' I asked.

Still frowning, Bevis nodded. 'But I don't see what that has ...'

'I'm coming to that,' I interrupted. ' I didn't tell you the truth about what he said that night when I phoned him. Not the full truth, at least.'

'Go on.'

'He saw something—on the morning of the fire.' I was watching him closely, to see his reactions. 'He saw a car, Bev, driving down the lane at such a pace that it almost put him in the ditch, just a couple of minutes before he rescued me.'

His eyes held mine. In them I saw surprise, then dawning horror as he realised the implications of what I had told him.

'Why didn't he say something before?' he demanded.

'He wasn't sure if it was important.'

'Well, why the devil didn't you say something? If it's true, Pam ... Good God, it puts an entirely diferent light on ...'

'Yes, I know. If that car was leaving my cottage, who was it, and what had he been doing?'

'Are you telling me the milkman saw Alan Hart ...'

'No! No, he didn't see anything clearly. It was dark, just before a storm. All he could tell me was that it was a pale-coloured car. He did say that it could have been white, or blue, but . . .'

'Then what made you ask about Alan Hart? Are you sure you don't remember anything about what went on between the two of you?'

'It's all as blank as it ever was. I just thought, perhaps he might have reasons to . . .'

'To kill you.' Bevis's voice was expressionless. 'That is what we're talking about, isn't it? But there could be a dozen people with pale-coloured cars who . . . Once you start thinking along those lines . . . James Summerton drives a yellow Sprite, for instance.'

'And your car,' I said quietly, 'is white.'

'Exactly. And there's mother's pale blue . . .' He stopped, studied my face, and added in a diferent tone, 'Am I your number one suspect?'

'Not any more,' I said.

A spasm of anger crossed his face and disappeared, leaving him thoughtful. 'I suppose I can't blame you. In your shoes, I'd have thought the same. I had motive, means . . . but not the opportunity. I was in the office all that day, from nine onwards. I may have detested you, Pam, but not to that extent. You do know that that clause in the will wouldn't stand up in court? Though I suppose

I might conceivably have wanted to get rid of you before you could contest the will. How are you to tell?'

'Instinct. If I had really believed it might be you, I wouldn't have told you any of this. At first we couldn't see who else would have cause, but, as you say, there might be a dozen people . . .'

'We?' Bevis repeated, eyes narrowed. 'You haven't told mother . . .'

'No, of course not! I . . . told James, this evening.'

'I see.'

I had a feeling he was having difficulty controlling his temper. He sat with his head bent, staring at the carpet, and said eventually. 'It would have been ideal for him, if I had been the one. He wouldn't want to look beyond the obvious. With me out of the way . . .'

'Yes?'

He looked up at me soberly. 'If I tell you, remember it's only the impression I got—from my jaundiced position on the sidelines. I was nobody, the working-class up-start . . .'

'Maybe that allowed you to see things more clearly,' I said.

'Or perhaps I was prejudiced, an inverted snob, jealous . . .' He sighed. 'I wish I knew, Pam. But it seemed to me that James Summerton was only interested in you because of what you might be worth some day. His people are upper-crust, but these days the upper class isn't rich any more, and besides, James is a younger son. What there is will go to his older brother. So his only hope of retaining the life-style he enjoys so much is to marry a rich woman.'

'But I'm not rich,' I objected. 'I'm up to my ears in debt.'

'Only until mother dies. And you're attractive enough to make the waiting worth while. Of course, I may be wrong. Perhaps he's just madly in love with you, couldn't forget you, and perhaps I'm just a miserable cynic. Has he even mentioned your father's money?'

'Several times,' I said ruefully. 'He even asked about the terms of the will, though I didn't tell him what they were ... There must be something wrong with me. I seem to attract all the wrong type of men. A revolutionist, a married man, and now a fortune hunter.'

'You can't be sure about Alan Hart,' Bevis reminded me. 'Just because you have a photograph of him needn't necessarily mean you were having an affair with him. If there had been some emotional relationship, surely he'd have tried to get in touch with you by now?'

'Unless the affair had ended—perhaps with bitter recriminations. Perhaps I threatened to tell his wife, or something.'

'Which brings us back to the car in the lane,' Bevis said. 'You do realise that there's only one way we'll find out the truth about that?'

'The police?' I said sadly.

'I'm afraid so. I'll telephone them first thing in the morning. It didn't seem necessary while it looked like an accident, or . . . something.'

'Or suicide,' I amended.

'Now who told you that?' he asked furiously.

'I didn't need telling! I'm not stupid. It is a possibility. But if it was that, it isn't about to happen again. I'd be grateful if you'd assure your mother of that. All day she's been keeping an anxious eye on me, as if she was afraid I might cut my wrists the minute I was out of her sight. It's a wonder she trusted me with the secateurs—I've been pruning and spraying roses, in case you're interested.'

'Doesn't this business about the car worry you?' Bevis asked.

'Yes, it does, if I think about it. So I've stopped thinking about it, the same way I've stopped thinking about my lost memory. I'm quite good at being an ostrich.'

'But you do agree that we ought to inform the police?'

'I suppose so,' I said dubiously. 'But I can't tell them anything.'

'You can't, but Alfred Davies can. The police are the only ones with the facilities to discover the truth.'

My mood had become one of fatalism. Since I had no hope of ever understanding the puzzle by myself, with no memories to aid me,

I must be content to sit back and let happen what would. The situation was too complex by now for me to control.

*   *   *

I had just finished dressing the following morning when there was a knock on my door and Bevis's voice asked, 'Are you awake?'

'Yes,' I called. 'Come in.'

He closed the door behind him and leaned on it, watching me brush my hair. 'I've been on to the police. They're going to contact Alfred Davies first, then they want to see the cottage, and you.'

'Me?' I put down the brush and turned to him in consternation. 'But didn't you tell them I can't . . .'

'Of course I told them. They want to talk to you, just the same. I came up to see you because . . . I'd like to keep mother out of it for as long as possible. She'll only worry. I'd rather find out what the police have to say before we tell her anything. What do you think?'

'Oh, I agree. It might easily turn out that that car had nothing to do with me. Perhaps a game-keeper, or a forester . . . There's no point in worrying Marjorie unnecessarily. I don't know why you had to tell her you suspected I'd tried to kill myself, Bev.'

'That was for her protection as much as

yours. I wanted her to know it was a possibility.'

'Was?' I queried with a grimace. 'It's still as likely an answer as any. We shall never know what really happened, unless I get my memory back. I was the only person there at the time, unless . . .'

'Unless you had a visitor, driving a pale-coloured car, who left in a hurry.'

'Back to square one. All we seem to do is talk round and round in circles.'

Bevis grinned suddenly. 'Your geometry's a bit confused. Or is it your metaphors? But I know what you mean. Still, it's a good thing we can talk about it, even if we get nowhere. It's an improvement on a few years ago, when you wouldn't talk about yourself at all . . . So, as far as mother's concerned, we're just going to the cottage to start cleaning-up operations. She's busy fixing some food for us to take. Did James say what time he was coming?'

'No, he didn't, but he knows where to find us. What time are you picking Lorraine up?'

'Oh, ah . . .' He blinked, shifting his gaze away from me. 'She wasn't feeling too good yesterday. I said if she didn't call me I'd assume she wasn't well enough to come.' Shrugging, he met my eyes again. 'She hasn't called.'

'I'm sorry,' I said, concerned. 'What's wrong with her?'

'Cold coming, I think. Nothing to worry

about. Are you coming down for breakfast now?'

Marjorie had packed a basket with enough food for a dozen people. She saw us off with instructions to me not to overtire myself.

'And I'll look for your ring,' she called as we climbed into the white Viva. ' I'm sure it can't be far away. Have a good day.'

'Ring?' Bevis enquired.

I showed him my left hand. 'I lost it yesterday. We think it must have come off when I was gardening. We couldn't find it in the house.'

The trees were now noticeably turning to gold and red, glowing in the mellow autumn sunlight. Although I was not particularly looking forward to being at the cottage—and talking with the police—I had managed not to think too closely about it until we slowed and turned into the long, shadowy lane, when the menace I had felt before seemed to reach out for me, making me aware that there might be real danger lurking somewhere. 'Don't go wandering in lonely places,' James' voice said in my head. 'For God's sake be careful—of everyone.'

There was a car already parked outside the cottage. We both saw it at the same time, but it was Bevis who recognised it.

'Well, now,' he said under his breath, bringing the Viva up beside the rusty Austin. 'Here's a turn-up for the book.'

'Whose car is it?' I asked.

'Someone we talked about only last night. Look at the colour. Beige.'

With a chill shock of alarm I realised what he meant. 'Alan Hart?' I breathed. 'Oh, Bev ... What's he doing here? I can't face him.'

'Why not? You don't know him, do you?' He watched me closely, saying again, 'Do you?'

'No!' I shook my head wildly. 'But what's he doing here, if ...'

'Let's find out, shall we?' He got out of the car, bent to look at me. ' Come on, Pam. Don't you want to find out a bit more?'

'No, I don't think I do,' I said dully, but I knew that I had to. I joined Bevis by the Austin. It had a big dent in its front bumper. I had never seen it before in my life—as far as I remembered.

'Good morning!' Bevis called.

Looking round I saw Alan Hart—immediately recognisable from his photograph—standing on the gravel path between the shrubs. He had paused there uncertainly, with no trace of the wicked grin, a large raffia-work shopping bag hanging heavily from one hand. He wore old trousers, a check shirt, an ancient suede jacket. He looked extremely embarrassed.

'Is it something to do with the shop?' Bevis asked in a pleasant tone. 'I must have

113

forgotten to tell you that Pamela's staying at the Hall with us.'

'No, it's not the shop.' Alan Hart's voice was very deep, melodic. He moved down the path with the air of one deciding to confront an unpleasant situation. 'I've been tending the garden for Mrs. Lane, using it as an allotment. Trish and I only have a flat. No garden of our own, you see. I've been . . . harvesting. I didn't realise you'd be here today.'

'You ought to have mentioned it the other day,' Bevis said. 'What have you got?'

Alan Hart, shorter by a few inches than my step-brother, his dark, unruly hair lifting in the slight breeze, opened his basket, displaying a couple of yellow and green marrows, some beetroot, tomatoes, and a couple of handfuls of pea pods, past their best.

'I didn't think you'd be wanting any,' he said, looking directly at me for the first time. There was a faint red flush on his cheeks, and worry in the fine dark eyes.

I had been afraid of meeting him, but now I couldn't think why. He was a stranger to me. 'You're welcome to whatever there is,' I said. 'I had a feeling it wasn't me who kept the garden so tidy.'

He looked puzzled, as though he didn't believe that I could not know him.

'How long have you been doing it?' Bevis asked.

'What—today?' With an effort, Alan Hart

114

took his eyes off me. 'Oh—I see what you mean. About . . . well, since the spring. Mrs. Lane advertised for a gardener, but we agreed I should have it for my own use, giving her a share of the produce. Only . . . I'm going to have to give it up, Mrs. Lane. My wife and I are moving. We'll have our own garden.' His gaze was back on my face, searching every feature.

Embarrassed, I looked away, down at the ground between us. 'I'm leaving the cottage, anyway.'

'Oh?' He dug in the pocket of his disreputable jacket, bringing out a key. 'You'd better have this, then.'

As I took the key, Bevis said quietly, 'Why did you need a key to the house?'

'In case Mrs. Lane was out. The key to the shed is kept indoors. All the tools are in the shed. I've cleaned them, and locked everything up. Well . . . I'll say goodbye.'

'One thing puzzles me,' Bevis said, leaning on the car door to prevent the other man from closing it. 'Was my sister using The Wishing Well as an outlet for the things she makes *before* you started doing her garden?'

'No.' The deep voice was suddenly hoarse. Nervously he cleared his throat, watching me with a little frown between his brows. 'When I saw her work, I knew my wife would be interested. I introduced them. Does it matter?'

'Just filling in a few gaps,' Bevis said,

115

releasing the door.

With an alacrity that spoke of his eagerness to get away from us, Alan Hart sent his car reversing in a wide swift arc that sent the dust flying, then shifted into forward gear and was gone.

I released my held-in breath with a sigh.

'Relieved?' Bevis asked mockingly.

'Yes, I am. I wondered what you were going to ask next.'

'You didn't feel any ... affinity, with him? No breathless attraction?'

'The only thing I found especially attractive was his voice,' I said. 'He doesn't mean a thing to me, not now. Perhaps he never did.'

'Then why was he so jumpy? And why couldn't he take his eyes off you?'

'I don't know, Bev,' I said sadly. 'I wish I could tell you the answers, but I can't. Anyway, he's gone now. If ever there was anything between us, it's obviously over.'

'But was it over before?' he asked in a quiet, meaningful voice. 'Was it over as calmly as it appears? If he's only your gardener, why do you keep a framed photograph of him in your room?'

'I don't know!'

He touched my shoulder gently, soothingly. 'Rhetorical questions, Pam. I'm sorry. But you do realise that we'll have to tell the police about him?'

'Oh, we can't!' I cried. 'His wife ...'

'He should have thought about her sooner. We can't afford to pick and choose what we tell the police. They have to know everything. But they do know how to be discreet. Hart's wife need never know anything about it—if he's innocent. And if he's not ... well, he ought to be caught.'

'Before he tries again?' I asked, and saw the swift, worried look he gave me. 'Oh, I'm aware of the possibilities. If I was attacked, then somewhere in my head I must know who did it. When I remember—*if* I remember ... James pointed out that I may still be in danger.'

'James did?' Bevis's eyes flashed with fury. 'He was stupid to frighten you.'

'Or warn me, put me on my guard.'

'He should have talked to *me* about it. How could he know what effect it would have on you? The state you've been in ... But you needn't worry. Nobody's going to lay a finger on you while I'm around.'

He looked so belligerent that I had to smile. 'You've changed your tune a bit. A few days ago you couldn't have cared less what happened to me.'

'It's mother I'm thinking about. She'd expect me to protect you. Damn it all, you're my step-sister!'

He led the way into the cottage. The three cats were all in the yard and had evidently been fed by Alan Hart. The empty catfood tins were still on the kitchen table.

117

'For a gardener, he makes himself pretty much at home,' Bevis growled. 'How about some coffee?'

'Where are you going?' I asked as he opened the door to the living-room.

'To size up the damage, plan where to start.'

'But I thought we weren't going to . . .'

'We're not. I don't intend to touch anything, don't worry. But when the police have finished the job will still have to be done.'

Waiting for the kettle to boil, I stood at the window watching the cats groom themselves in a sunny corner. The window needed washing. Perhaps that would be something I could do while we waited. Sitting around in that place, even with Bevis for company, would be unnerving.

I was glad when the kettle boiled and I had made the coffee, giving me an excuse to call my step-brother back to the kitchen. But as I opened my mouth I heard him call me, from upstairs.

'Pam! Pam, come up here a minute.'

Forcing myself to it, I ran across the corner of the desolate living-room and hurried along the hall, up the stairs. Bevis was in my bedroom, regarding me quizzically.

'Am I crazy, or did we leave that photograph on the chest of drawers?'

'Yes, we did.' The photograph of Alan Hart was gone. Puzzled, I looked around the room.

'It's not here,' Bevis assured me. 'We left

118

this room together the other night and we haven't been back since. Only one person has been in the cottage.'

I stared at him. 'Alan Hart? You think he . . .'

'Removed the evidence?' Bevis finished for me. 'I don't know who else would have bothered, do you?'

CHAPTER SIX

It seemed that Alan Hart, in an effort to prevent himself from appearing to be involved in my life, had taken his photograph from my bedroom. However, Bevis said that he couldn't have taken the frame, too. It was too bulky to go in a pocket and we had seen the contents of the basket he carried. So Bevis was carrying out a search for the frame.

It didn't appear to be in the house.

'Your coffee will be stone cold,' I told him as he crossed the yard to open the shed.

'I'll make some more when I've finished,' he said.

Curiosity drew me to the shed door. There was a tea-chest crammed full of junk, garden tools arranged neatly against the wall, a work-bench with a vice attached to one end, and a lady's cycle—with new white-wall tyres. I owed money to the local garage for those tyres, I

119

thought with a sigh.

'What did I tell you?' Triumphantly, Bevis drew the picture-frame from beneath a piece of sacking in the tea-chest. One corner was broken and the glass was cracked, but it was certainly the same frame which had held the photograph of Alan Hart. 'If we hadn't arrived when we did, we might never have known who took it. Why was he so anxious to get hold of it?'

'Perhaps he thought it might remind me of something. But it needn't mean that he's the one who . . .'

'No, but it doesn't look very good for him, does it? The police will be interested in this.'

'Will they believe us? It's only our word against his now.'

'That's true, but at least two of us saw that photograph. They'll have to look into it. I'll leave the frame here, in case they want to see it.'

Returning into the warm golden sunlight, I closed my eyes, breathing deeply of the fresh air, the autumnal smell of ripe things that came on the breeze.

'Why does everything have to be so complicated?' I sighed to the world in general.

'God knows,' Bevis said, in such an odd tone that I opened my eyes and surprised a look on his face that was gone before I could identify it. Sorrow, perhaps? Why?

'I'm really ready for that coffee now,' he

said as he made for the kitchen. 'Do you want some?'

'I wouldn't say no. How long do you think the police will be?'

'No idea. Why, are you getting restless?'

'It's just this place. I can't relax here. I keep remembering that dream. It was so real.'

He paused with the coffee jar in his hand. 'What dream?'

'Didn't I tell you? Oh—no, come to think of it, it was James I told.'

'You tell him a hell of a lot too much!' Bevis said angrily. 'So what was this dream about?'

I recounted it in detail, for it was still clear in my mind—the living-room bright with colour, the vague figure ... As I stopped talking I glanced at the inner door, my throat thick with remembered fear.

'Now why didn't you tell me before?' Bevis demanded. 'Why tell James and not me?'

'Because he was friendly and you weren't. I couldn't talk to you, not then. You'd only have said I was making it up. Anyway, it's not revelant, is it? It was just a dream.'

'Yes, but with your memory not functioning normally ...' He broke off as heavy footsteps came thudding down the path at the side of the cottage. I saw James rush past the window, then the door flew open and he stood there looking from one to the other of us, breathing heavily.

'Well, if it isn't the white tornado in person,'

Bevis said drily. 'What's the rush, James?'

Glaring at him, James turned furiously to me. 'Are you crazy? Why didn't you wait for me? I thought I told you . . .'

'Maybe she doesn't take orders from you,' Bevis broke in.

James dropped into a chair beside me, taking my hand. 'Are you all right?'

'I'm fine,' I said, as another shadow darkened the doorway. To my surprise, Lorraine stood there, dressed for dirty work.

'Hi,' she greeted, her eyes resting on Bevis with an almost defiant expression. He, I noted, was staring at her in blank shock.

'My father gave me a lift to the lane end,' she told him levelly. 'Then James came past and picked me up.'

'You said you'd call,' Bevis said flatly.

'I changed my mind. Woman's privilege. How's the work going?'

'It's not.' With that flat statement Bevis went to get out more cups.

Lorraine glanced at me. 'Why not?'

'It's a long story,' I said. 'I'm glad you're feeling better.'

'Better?' She pulled her mouth awry, glancing at Bevis. 'Did he say I was ill? My, my, what a liar you are, Bev.'

'Would you rather I had told her the truth?' he demanded grimly.

'That we had a row? Why not? I'm sure Pamela knows such things happen. I decided to forgive you, anyway, and come along to help, but if you're not working . . . What *have* you been doing?'

'That,' said James, 'is what I would like to know.'

'We're waiting for the police,' I explained, making them both turn startled faces in my direction. 'You were right, James. It's the only sensible thing to do. When I told Bev about the car . . .'

'You *told* him?' James asked in a horrified voice.

'Yes, I did. It seemed . . .'

Bevis interrupted me, brushing me aside as he stood before James, bristling. 'Now just hold on! I'm bloody slow today, aren't I? Is that why you came rushing in here as if the hounds of hell were on your tail? You thought she might be in danger from me? Is that it?'

'You're the obvious one!' James stood up, face to grim face with Bevis, both their hands clenched. 'Who else stands to gain a fortune?'

'You do—if she's stupid enough to marry you,' Bevis raged. 'But she wasn't that stupid, was she? She saw through you a long time ago. Maybe you came back, before the fire. Maybe she told you to go to hell. Maybe it was *your* car in the lane that day.'

'Bevis!' I forced my way between them and James stepped back, near the open door.

'No, let him go on,' he said roughly. 'Can't you see? He's just trying to draw attention

123

away from himself. But however much mud he slings, some of it will stick to him. He has a few thousand crisp green motives.'

My hand was against Bevis's chest. I could feel him shaking as he fought to hold down his temper and I was afraid. The hatred flowing between them was like a high-voltage current.

'You're accusing me of attempted murder,' Bevis said in a hoarse voice. 'Summerton ... get out of here. And stay away.'

'And if I don't?' James taunted. 'What will you do? Knock me out and leave me to burn, like ...'

I was pushed aside, cannoned into Lorraine. Clutching her, I heard the awful sound of fist on flesh and turned in time to see James staggering backwards into the yard. He fell heavily, sending one of the cats' saucers skittering madly. As I rushed into the yard, the three cats woke up and streaked away.

James' lower lip was split and bleeding. I bent over him, helping him up, and from behind me, Lorraine said coldly, 'I hope you're proud of yourself, Bev Heyman. You're nothing but a bully! If I hadn't seen it for myself I'd never have believed it. I was right yesterday, wasn't I?'

There was no reply. Glancing round, I saw Bevis examining his right hand.

'Wasn't I?' Lorraine insisted.

'Oh ... go to hell!' Bevis growled, and returned to the kitchen.

'I wish I'd never come,' Lorraine said to nobody in particular. 'I ought to have known better. James ... will you please take me home? We don't *have* to stay here, do we?'

'I can't leave Pamela here alone,' James objected, dabbing at his lip with a handkerchief.

'I'm not alone,' I said quietly. 'Bevis is here with me. No—don't say it, James. You've said quite enough already. The best thing you can do is to take Lorraine home as she asks. Unless you particularly want to speak with the police.'

He looked at me askance. 'I've nothing to be afraid of. I was in Sheffield when that fire started and I can prove it.'

'And Bevis was at the office,' I informed him. 'He was, wasn't he, Lorraine?'

She glanced venomously at the cottage. 'I couldn't swear to it, so don't ask. Whatever's going on, I want no part of it. Let's get out of here, James.'

'You're sure?' James asked me anxiously.

'Yes, I'm sure.'

'When shall I see you?'

'You know where I live.'

'Tonight? Have dinner with me. Somewhere quiet, away from all this.'

'I'll see,' I said. 'Phone me at the Hall later.'

When they had gone, I went slowly back into the kitchen, not knowing what to expect. Bevis stood in the doorway to the living-room, leaning on the jamb as he stared at the desolation beyond. His whole demeanour expressed dejection.

'Bev?' I touched his arm, but he shrugged me off, saying roughly, 'Leave me alone, can't you? You made it quite obvious whose side you're on, rushing to his aid like that.'

'Only because he was hurt. He was asking for it. He had no right to say those things. You both completely lost control. And it's not a question of choosing sides . . . Bev?' I ducked down so that I could see his face and he turned abruptly away, going to stare out of the window. I watched him, worried. There had been tears in his eyes.

'What's wrong?' I asked. 'Is it Lorraine? She'll come round when she understands . . .'

'Oh, for God's sake!' he exploded. 'Shut up, Pam!'

Not understanding the emotions he was battling with, I subsided, and noticed the coffees still steaming on the table. I sat down, putting sugar into one of the cups.

'Don't let this one get cold,' I said in a low voice. 'Come and sit down Bev.'

He rubbed his face with his hands and obeyed, taking the chair on the opposite side of the table. He looked at his coffee as he stirred it, not at me.

My pulse was still hammering with tension and my hand was trembling as I sipped my drink. Naturally he was upset, having allowed

126

his temper to get the better of him, and quarrelling with Lorraine, but there seemed to be more to it, something I couldn't fathom.

'Do you want to talk about it?' I asked.

'No.'

'You've skinned your knuckles.'

'Yes.'

Silence again. Outside somewhere, a blackbird was giving its warning call, the shrill 'chip-chip-chip-chip' sounding loud and so insistent that I got up and closed the back door against it.

'Are you ready for some lunch?' I asked.

'I'm not hungry.' Tossing down the last of the coffee, he stood up, still avoiding my eyes. 'I think I'll go for a stroll. Not far. If the police come, tell them I won't be long.'

I choked back the desire to beg him not to leave me alone. 'All right, Bev.'

He must have noticed my tone, for he glanced at me. 'I won't be far away. There's nothing to be afraid of. There's nobody around. If I hear a car coming I'll come straight back. I just want a few minutes to myself. Is that too much to ask?'

'No, of course not. You go. I'll be all right. I thought . . . the windows need washing. That'll keep me busy. You go.'

He regarded me steadily for a moment, as if wondering whether to change his mind, but his unhappiness won the day. He muttered, 'Thanks,' and went out.

Left alone in that place with its creepy feeling of unremembered horrors, I applied myself with vigour to the task of window washing. I found a bucket and a piece of ragged but clean towel and went out to the yard.

The window was dusty, cobwebs draping the corners. I washed down glass and paintwork, the hairs on the back of my neck prickling so that occasionally I glanced round at the garden behind me, which lay still in the sunlight. The feeling of being watched was just part of my general unease, I told myself.

Having dealt with the windows of kitchen and sewing room, I took the bucket to the front of the house and began to sluice down the living-room window. Like the others it was made up of small square panes, though here there were four sections instead of two. With the sun shining brightly on the shrubs behind me it was easy to avoid looking through the glass into that room that I hated.

There was a movement in the glass. Startled, I turned to look at the front garden, and behind me a voice said, 'You'd better come in.'

It was a woman's voice, in the room behind me, muffled but still clear enough to hear. I froze in cold surprise, slowly turning to look through the window. A human shape moved behind the reflections.

And as I looked she screamed, 'No! Bevis,

no!' flung up her arms—and fell.

I put my hands either side of my face, to see more clearly, though my heart was beating crazily and black shapes whirled about my head. It couldn't be real. I saw the woman lying on the floor, her face turned towards me.

It was myself. There was no one else in the room.

Feeling sick, I turned away and tripped over the bucket. I flung out my hands to save myself and caught a rose bush, the thorns tearing into my flesh as I landed in an ungainly heap among leaves and weeds and soft earth. Sobbing, I picked myself up and ran blindly down the path, into the road, veering away from Bevis's car as if it were a monster. Not knowing where I was going, I ran on down the lane.

I didn't even see the green sedan until it stopped, directly in front of me. I almost ran into it. I stood swaying.

'Are you all right?' asked the man who climbed out of the car. 'Miss? What's wrong, miss?'

'Mrs.,' I corrected, gasping for breath. Sanity was coming back to me. I felt very cold. 'Mrs. Lane. I'm sorry. I'm not well. Seeing things. That place . . .'

'You're Pamela Lane?' He peered at my face. 'We were coming to see you. Let us take you back home.'

Taking my arm, he led me to the rear door

of the car and put me inside, himself resuming the passenger seat. Another man was driving.

'Quite a state you've got yourself into,' the passenger commented, nodding at my hands and arms, which were bleeding in several places.

'An argument with a rose bush,' I said, attempting a laugh. 'I frightened myself. It's that cottage. I was nearly killed there.'

'Yes, I know. Your brother told us. It was a nasty business, by all accounts. You don't remember any of it?'

'No, nothing.'

We were pulling up outside the cottage.

'Is that your car?' the man asked.

'My brother's. He went for a walk. I was cleaning windows. I seemed to see ... what happened that day. It's happened before. A dream about being attacked. I don't know why I ran. It was stupid.'

'Don't worry about it,' he said comfortably. 'Let's get you inside.'

I let him lead me towards the cottage, the second man following. The back door was open, as I had left it, but I was suddenly terrified of going inside. What I had seen had been so real. Suppose she was still lying there. She—I.

At a nod from my companion, the second man went ahead, looking all round the ground floor of the cottage.

'Nobody here,' he reported. 'Come in, Mrs.

Lane. There's nothing to be afraid of. Sit down and relax.'

I did so. The first man leaned on the edge of the table. He was dark-haired, personable, with blue eyes that reminded me of James. 'Tell me what you saw,' he requested.

'Myself. In there. I was letting somebody in, though I saw no one else. And then ... she screamed. *I* screamed—my image. And fell. I saw myself quite clearly lying there. But there was nobody else in the room.'

'You think this might be a buried memory?'

'I don't know. The dream I had was almost the same, but I don't know. I can't remember.'

With that, Bevis was at the door. He had evidently been hurrying.

'Police?' he asked.

'Yes,' the dark man agreed. 'You're Mr. Heyman? How do you do. I'm John Anderson, Detective Inspector, and this is Sergeant Carter. Your sister's a bit upset, I'm afraid. She seems to have had some sort of ... waking dream, about an attack on her, here in the cottage.'

'Again?' Bevis knelt in front of me, reaching for my hands, looking up at me with concern. 'Oh, Pam ... I shouldn't have left you. How do you feel?'

'Fine,' I said. It was almost true, now that he was here, despite what that apparition had screamed.

'We've had a long talk with Mr. Davies,' the

Inspector said, offering cigarettes which we both refused. He lit one for himself, squinting against the smoke. 'We've also been to the hospital and spoken with the doctor who tended your sister. According to him, the blow on her head might have been caused by a fall, or it might have been done by an assailant, though he did say that at the time he accepted it as an accident.

'As for the car that the milkman saw, it's entirely possible it has no connection with this case. We'll make enquiries, of course, but on such a vague description . . . Unless your sister happens to remember who might have had a grudge.'

'I might,' Bevis said. 'And I have a white car, and motive enough . . . But I'm afraid I was at my office all that morning, though I suppose I could conceivably have come here before going to work. If the milkman was only just coming it must have been early.'

Anderson smiled. 'Half past eleven, according to Mr. Davies. This is his second round of the day, and the last house on the list. I appreciate your frankness, Mr. Heyman, but it's not much help.'

'You'll check it, I hope?'

'Yes, we will. But unless you've any more constructive suggestions . . .'

Bevis was still holding my hands. Or perhaps I was holding his. His eyes asked a question and I shook my head. I was in no state to make decisions.

Slowly, my-step-brother rose to his feet. 'It's difficult,' he told the Inspector. 'With my sister not remembering anything ... I know very little about her private life. All we can do is guess, and I don't like to involve someone who may be innocent.'

'We can't get any further without your help,' Anderson replied. 'Only by collecting as many facts as possible can we hope to get at the truth. That often means questioning innocent people, if only to eliminate them from our enquiries.'

Bevis sighed. 'All right. But please be careful. We don't want to upset any apple carts. There is a man who ... well, we suspect he may have been having some sort of relationship with my sister. She had a photograph of him in her room. The man himself says that he only came here to use the garden—as a kind of allotment. He was here today and we talked to him. I don't think he was being entirely frank with us. And when he had gone we discovered that the photograph of him was missing. I found the frame hidden in the shed.'

'Show me?' Anderson invited.

Wearily Bevis led the way across the yard. Despite his earlier confidence, he wasn't enjoying this at all. I was left alone in the kitchen, hearing their voices but not bothering to listen to what they were saying. In the living-room Sergeant Carter was poking about. I still felt chilled to the marrow.

If I was starting to hallucinate, was I going mad? Was my buried memory playing havoc with the workings of my mind? And what had it meant? Why had my mirror image cried Bevis's name? Nothing in the world would make me believe that Bevis had tried to hurt me. But perhaps my subconscious believed it.

I heard the two men leave the shed and stand talking in subdued voices. Talking about me, I didn't doubt. Were they discussing my sanity?

For the second time I noticed the state my hands were in. I went to the sink and turned on the tap to wash my hands, wincing at the pain brought by soap and water. The inside of one wrist was badly cut and there was a long, bleeding scratch up my forearm. What with cats and rosebushes, I seemed fated to be torn to pieces.

' . . . check into it for you,' Anderson was saying as he came through the door. 'Though I can't make any promises. With so little to go on, we'll be pretty lucky to find the driver of that car. Maybe the local paper would help. I'll see what I can do . . . Feeling better, Mrs. Lane?'

'Yes, thank you. I'm sorry about . . .'

'Oh, that's all right. We quite understand. You're under an enormous strain. We'll do our best to put your mind at rest—about this

134

mysterious car if nothing else. I don't think you have any need to worry. Do you mind if I have a look around?'

'Help yourself,' I said, reaching for the towel.

We could hear the two policemen conferring in the living-room, moving through to the hall.

'Are you sure you're all right?' Bevis asked worriedly.

'Yes, I'm fine now. Will you pass me my bag, please? I think I ought to take another pill.'

'You need something on your hands, too. They look terribly sore. Maybe there's some ointment somewhere.'

He began to search the cupboards while I filled a cup with water and swallowed the tranquilliser, hoping it would be effective. Inside I was atwitch with nerves. Bevis found a tube of antiseptic cream and made me sit down while he gently applied the cooling salve to my hurts. I could easily have done it myself, but I was grateful for his care.

'Your post comes late,' Inspector Anderson remarked with a smile, tossing an envelope on to the table. 'Well, I think we've seen about all we want to see for now. If you remember anything else that might help, you know where to find us.'

'Can we get it cleaned up now?' Bevis asked.

'No reason why not. Thank you for your cooperation. Goodbye, Mrs, Lane. I hope you feel better soon.'

Bevis followed them out and the three men stood talking briefly by the corner of the house. My eyes were drawn to the living-room door, which stood open. Slowly, I got up and walked across to it, to assure myself there was no one there. I half expected the prostrate form to materialise before my eyes, but nothing came. There was only the carpet, filthy now, and the skeleton of the couch.

'Don't think about it,' Bevis said gently from behind me. 'It was my fault. I shouldn't have left you.'

'He didn't believe it, did he?' I replied. 'He thinks I'm just a hysterical female imagining things. They won't try very hard to find that car.'

'Are you so sure it's important?'

I turned to face him. 'Aren't you?'

Bevis shook his head sorrowfully. 'I honestly don't know what to think. Haven't you opened your letter?' Picking up the envelope, he studied the postmark. 'It's from Dorset.'

'Open it,' I instructed. 'Read it out to me.'

With a lift of one eyebrow, Bevis obeyed. The letter was from someone named Ellen Forrester, thanking me for my letter, in which I had told her about her daughter's visit to me. She went on at length about how friendly she had been with my mother and how she would love to see Derbyshire again and ended by

136

inviting me to have a holiday at her home.

'Mean anything?' Bevis asked.

'Not a thing.' I held out my hand for the letter and for a moment, as I saw the writing, it seemed to try to convey something to me. But the feeling faded almost at once. It was not going to open any doors. All the same, I folded it carefully, replaced it in the envelope, and put it in my handbag.

'Do you want to go home now?' Bevis asked.

I glanced at the basket of food which stood on the fridge. 'Marjorie will wonder why we haven't eaten anything. It's way past lunchtime.'

'Well, shall we have a meal first? It's up to you.'

Much as I detested the thought of staying at the cottage, I was more concerned about worrying Marjorie. We laid the table and sat down to a late lunch of cold meats and salad, talking only when it was necessary. Gradually it seeped through my self-indulgent moodiness that Bevis was being unusually quiet, but I said nothing until we were clearing the table.

' Didn't the walk help?'

It took a moment for him to realise what I meant, then he pulled his mouth awry. 'It calmed me down. I'm ashamed of myself. Thank God the police didn't arrive earlier and find us brawling. Though I suppose James

137

might sue for assault and battery. Lori will be only too glad to testify for him.'

'She didn't mean, what she said,' I reassured. 'She was upset. You'll make it up next time you meet.'

'I wouldn't bank on it.'

'Why not? Did you have a serious quarrel? . . . But if it had been that bad she wouldn't have come today. She said she'd forgiven you.'

'That was big of her,' Bevis said bitterly, 'considering she started the row.'

'What was it about? Or shouldn't I ask?'

'You shouldn't ask.'

'Oh. Sorry.' I busied myself with hot water and liquid detergent, beginning to wash the dishes and stack them on the drainer while Bevis took up the tea towel to dry them.

'What exactly happened this morning?' he asked. 'What were you doing when you had this "waking dream"?'

'I'd rather not talk about that, either.'

'Were you frightened?'

'Yes, I was! Frightened enough to turn tail and run. For a few minutes I didn't know what I was doing. I'd have sworn there really was someone in the . . .' A shiver ran through me and I glanced at the inner door. It was closed now, hiding its secrets.

'Someone like you—who was being attacked?' Bevis persisted.

'I think so. I only saw the woman—myself.

But she shouted ...' I bit my lip, closing my eyes tight. I had promised myself never to repeat what that phantom had screamed.

'You heard words?' Bevis asked in surprise. 'What did she say?'

I had to tell him. It was something I couldn't prevent, as I had had to tell him the other things I knew, simply because I wanted to hear him tell me it wasn't so. In a hoarse whisper I said, 'She screamed, "Bevis, no!"'

There was a stunned silence. I couldn't look at him.

After what seemed like eternity he said in a voice devoid of expression, 'Why didn't you tell that to the police?'

'I couldn't!' Tears stung my eyes, squeezed out between my eyelids. 'It's crazy!'

'But in the back of your mind you still believe it could have been me.'

'No! No, that's just it. I don't believe it.'

'Pamela ...' He took hold of me by the shoulders, swung me to face him, put both hands either side of my face. 'Look at me!'

I opened my flooded eyes, blinking away the dazzle. He was very close, pain in the grey eyes that looked directly into mine.

'I swear to you I was not here that morning. By all I hold most dear. Believe me, Pamela!'

'I do,' I managed. 'Truly I do.'

'Oh, God!' Bevis said between his teeth. 'Don't cry. Please don't. I can't ...'

Unable to see him clearly, I was startled

139

when his lips met mine. He held my face tilted to his so that I couldn't move. I didn't want to move. A trembling had begun deep inside me, making me powerless against its sweetness as my whole being responded to him.

Abruptly he forced me away, holding me at arms' length, then let his hands fall and turned away. Grabbing up the tea towel with an impatient movement he went on with the business of drying dishes, saying gruffly, 'Let's get this finished. This place is getting on my nerves.'

And I, bewildered, obediently turned back to the sink.

CHAPTER SEVEN

Marjorie was surprised at our early return to the Hall. She had expected us to be working until early evening; so we were obliged to tell her the gist of the tale—about the pale-coloured car seen by the milkman, and the visit from the police. We did not mention Alan Hart, or my frightening vision. Neither did we speak of the fight, nor what had occurred between the two of us. Even so, what we did say worried Marjorie, who was far from stupid.

'I had a feeling there was something,' she said as we shared afternoon tea in the sitting-room. 'But at least we know the police will find out who that car belonged to. Oh, and . . . I've searched the garden, Pamela, but I can't find your ring. Phyllis and I looked everywhere. I'm sorry, darling, but it looks as though it's lost for good.'

'It can't be helped,' I said, looking at my bare left hand with its network of red scratches. I hadn't missed the ring at all.

Marjorie gasped as she saw my torn skin. 'Whatever did . . .' But the phone interrupted her. She jumped up to answer it, saying that it would be Mrs. Harris. The silence she left behind was profound.

'Who's Mrs. Harris?' I asked Bevis, not because I wanted to know.

'Something to do with the Women's Guild. Secretary, I think. Mother's on one of the committees.'

'Oh, I see.' Rising from my seat, I went to the window, looking out at a sky gone grey. Yellow leaves blew fitfully across the lawn. 'It's coming on to rain,' I said irrelevantly.

'Well, it is the first of October.'

'Is it? I hadn't realised. Summer's really gone, then. Do you like the autumn?'

'Sometimes. "Season of mists and mellow fruitfulness . . ."'

' "Close bosom-friend of the maturing sun",' I continued the quotation, which came from the lost reaches of my mind. Sighing, I turned back to the room. 'Why can't I remember anything important? Music, and now poetry.'

'It's a beginning,' Bevis said, and looked away as if he couldn't bear the sight of me.

Small talk. That was all we had exchanged since leaving the cottage. We were both striving for a return to our earlier relationship, the brother-sister easiness that had gone up in smoke in the flame of a moment's loss of control. But it had gone for good. We were aware of each other now, sexually aware, It wasn't a thing we could easily forget.

'It was James on the phone,' Marjorie said as she returned. She paused momentarily, sensing the atmosphere, looking from one to the other of us and deciding not to comment. 'He's booked a table at Vittorio's for eight o'clock, so he'll be calling for you at seven.'

I stared at her, astonished. 'Is that what he said? But ... I told him I didn't know if I wanted to go out. He was supposed to call and find out.'

'He's not the type to take "no" for an answer,' my step-mother said with a smile. 'It will do you good. You need a change. Try one of those dresses you left behind. Vittorio's is a very posh place. They have dancing. It's clever of James to have got a table there on a Saturday night. From all accounts it's usually full up. Now don't argue, Pamela. It's just what you need to take you out of yourself. Isn't it, Bevis?'

'Yes, it is,' he said quietly, giving me a glance full of meaning. 'You need a break.'

'There you are,' Marjorie triumphed. 'Off you go and have a long hot bath. You've lots of time to get ready. It's time we saw the old, glamorous Pamela again.'

I protested, but Marjorie was having none of it. She packed me off to get ready, telling me that if she was my age again she would leap at the chance of a dinner date with an attractive young man like James.

Reluctantly, I had a bath and let Marjorie lend me some perfume and make-up. I felt like a lamb being groomed for the slaughter. I tried on all of the evening dresses before deciding on one in a soft turquoise with a flowing skirt and halter neckline. It was the least revealing of the selection.

'You look lovely, darling,' Marjorie breathed. 'Just the way you always used to. You don't look any older, either. No, I mean it. James is going to be impressed. Now sit down and relax until he comes. He shouldn't be long. Tell you what—I'll fetch you a glass of sherry while you put the finishing touches. You're nervous, aren't you?'

'I feel quite sick,' I told her. 'I object to being bull-dozed, by James Summerton or anybody else.'

'Oh, nonsense! You'll enjoy yourself.'

Alone in my bedroom I brushed my hair with angry strokes. My stomach was in turmoil. The very last thing I wanted to do was to go out to dinner at a 'posh' restaurant. But perhaps Marjorie was right. Perhaps it would do me good.

'Are you decent?' Bevis's voice asked from beyond the door.

'Yes, come in.'

He paused in the doorway, a glass of sherry in one hand, looking me up and down with a stunned expression that made my cheeks flame.

'Here.' Collecting himself, he thrust the glass at me. Between us, we nearly spilled it. 'And this, too,' he added as he brought a book from behind his back and slapped it down on the dressing-table. 'You like poetry. Try Catullus.'

'Catullus?' I said blankly.

He gave me a furious glance. 'Yes, Catullus!' and he slammed from the room.

Astounded, I saw the book was a Dictionary of Quotations. I took a mouthful of sherry that went down like fire and made my eyes water before I put the glass aside and picked up the book, intrigued.

It was arranged alphabetically by author's name. I found the Cs and then 'Catullus. 84?-54? BC'. There were several quotations in Latin with English translations beneath. One of them had been heavily underlined in soft pencil.

'I hate, I love—the cause thereof
Belike you ask of me.

I do not know, but feel it's so,
And I'm in agony.'

The words blurred in front of me. My head swam. Dimly I heard the ringing of the doorbell.

'Pamela!' Marjorie's call echoed up the stairs. 'James is here.'

Slowly closing the book, I hid it beneath my pillow, my heart beating erratically. I had to have time to get used to the message in that poem, time to compose myself before I met Bevis again.

I felt rather theatrical going down the stairs with Marjorie's fur stole draped round my shoulders. My step-mother and James made an admiring audience, which made me hot with embarrassment.

'I'm lost for words,' James said, kissing my hand as if he, too, were acting in a play. 'You're stunning.'

I ought to have thanked him for the compliment, or expressed my dislike of his high-handed methods, but I couldn't concentrate. Bevis had appeared in the sitting-room doorway, lounging against the jamb wearing an expression of total disinterest. Marjorie was chattering, but I didn't hear what she said. Then I was aware of James' hand on my arm, firm and possessive, and I came back to reality.

' . . .home before dawn, I promise,' James

was laughing. 'But don't wait up, Mrs. Ennis. I'll take good care of her.'

'Make sure you do,' Marjorie replied, only half joking. 'Have a lovely time now.'

The night air was cool, with a light drizzle falling. James hurried me into his yellow sports car and it growled down the drive.

I hate, I love, I'm in agony. Oh, God!

'Alone at last,' James said with a grin. 'Did he give you an argument?'

'Who?' I asked blankly.

'Bevis. I thought I'd have another fight on my hands. Or has he come to the conclusion I'm not the villain of the piece after all?'

'Oh . . . yes. How's your lip?'

'Sore. What did the police have to say?'

'Not much. They're going to "make enquiries"—without much hope of success.'

'At least you've done the sensible thing.'

'Yes.'

It was half an hour before we drew up outside what looked like an ancient inn, its stone walls white-washed. Inside, the small dining-room was dimly lit by red-shaded lamps. Slender red candles waited on each table, and two white roses floating in a dish. There was a tiny dance floor, a subdued atmosphere, soft-voiced waiters dressed in immaculate black and white, and a trio playing quietly, dreamily,

James ordered aperitifs and we studied the huge menus. There was a vast choice, but I wasn't very hungry. Unable to make even that simple decision, I asked James to order for us both.

I remember very little of what we said that night. My mind wasn't on it. We ate, and in between courses we danced, very close. And we drank wine, which only increased my sense of apartness.

Eventually, as we sat down to pears nestling in lemon mousse with a sherry sauce. James said irritably, 'Where *are* you, Pamela?'

I looked across at him, numbed by wine. 'Vittorio's, isn't it?'

'You may be here physically, but mentally you're off somewhere. I thought you'd enjoy it here.'

'I am.'

'That isn't the impression I'm getting.' Angry, he looked very handsome, eyes flashing in his tanned face, shirt brilliant white in the candlelight, with a midnight blue bow tie that matched his dinner jacket.

For the life of me, I couldn't remember what we had been talking about.

His mood changed abruptly. Ardent blue eyes glowed as he reached across the table for my hand. 'Darling,' he said softly. 'What you really need is a complete break from the past, a new environment, new commitments. That's what I want to give you. Marry me, Pamela.'

'Marry you?' My voice was incredulous. 'But I hardly know you.'

'Of course you do!' he said tightly, then forced himself back to cajolery. 'You know me very well, darling. If you hadn't met David Lane we could have been married by now, probably with a family, and none of the bad things would have happened to you. We've wasted five years of our lives. Don't let's waste any more. We've been given a second chance. Let's take it, quickly.'

When I made no reply, he went on, 'You loved me once. I haven't changed. All I want is to take care of you. You don't belong at the Hall with those . . .' Whatever word he had been about to use, it wasn't complimentary to Marjorie and Bevis, but he bit it off and went on sweetly, 'You can't relax there. I've seen that. You're afraid of Bev, aren't you? He's not to be trusted, Pamela. Look at the way he went for me this morning. How can you hope to find peace in that house? Come to me, darling. Now.'

I couldn't think properly. No coherent thought would stay in my mind. Afraid of Bevis? That wasn't true. But I couldn't put any argument into words. All I knew was that the idea of rushing into marriage with James was ludicrous.

'I can't make a decision like that until I know . . . how I feel,' I said. 'I've lost my memory, or had you forgotten?'

'That doesn't matter to me,' James smiled, pressing the hand he held. 'I'll take you as you are. I love you, Pamela.'

'Why?' I asked.

The question surprised him, but after a moment's hesitation he replied smoothly, 'Because you're beautiful, and sweet. Because I love you. Who can give reasons?'

'It's not because I may inherit a lot of money one day?'

His mouth tightened with anger. 'No, it isn't! Who put that idea into your head? Bevis? But you know that he hates me. He'd do anything to come between us. Look at what he said this morning. As if *I* would ever dream of hurting you! That just shows what lengths he'll go to.'

I could hardly think at all. I felt so tired I could have put my head down on the table and gone to sleep.

'You needn't give me your answer now,' James said. 'Shall we have another dance while we wait for coffee?'

'If you like,' I said listlessly.

The small dancing area was crowded with couples barely moving, swaying in time to the slow music, some of them kissing, oblivious to their surroundings. James held me close against him, both arms round my waist, and I locked my hands behind his neck, letting my head droop on his shoulder. Sleep came nearer, sending my mind into orbit.

It must have been the tune that did it. 'Dream a little dream:' was 'our tune,' Paul's and mine. Paul. I held him tighter, wanting to keep him and knowing I couldn't. Such sadness filled me that tears soaked his jacket. I lifted my face blindly for one last bitter-sweet kiss, and breathed his name.

James jerked free of me with a force that brought me back to the present. As he hurried me back to the table, a flush of both hope and fear flooded my entire body. Paul. It had been Paul I was waiting for on the cliff-top that day, waiting so happily, until he arrived and told me he had fallen in love with someone else. But that was all I remembered, just that few minutes on the cliff. When it had happened, and where, I couldn't recall. But it seemed like a long, long time ago.

The waiter who brought our coffee melted away into the dimness.

'And who the devil is Paul?' James demanded.

'Someone I used to know. I'm sorry, James. For a moment I was back there with him. I think it's the wine.'

'Well, I hope you realise you've ruined my entire evening. Obviously I made a mistake bringing you here. You've forgotten how to conduct yourself in polite society, after living in that pig-sty of a cottage. You're as drunk as an owl. We'd better go before you make a complete fool of yourself. Drink your coffee.'

He was wrong. Perhaps I had been tipsy, but the shock of that few moments on the dance floor had sobered me, leaving a vague ache over my eyes. I was aware enough now to note the vicious tone of that last speech. They were hardly the words of an understanding lover.

Rain poured down outside. My hair was plastered down in the short walk to the car and I stepped in a puddle, my light sandals being no protection. But James didn't seem to care.

He didn't speak to me at all during our drive to the Hall, nor did he get out of the car when we drew up at the door, but merely said, 'Goodnight,' and shot away as if he were glad to get rid of me.

Shivering with the cold and wet, I let myself into the house. The light was still on in the sitting-room, so I went in there intending only to say goodnight before hurrying upstairs to get out of my damp clothes. Bevis was alone, standing with his back to the fireplace, looking grim and angry.

'Have you been waiting?' I asked.

'Not particularly. It's not that late.' Despite himself, it seemed, he was obliged to add, 'You're soaking! Is that his idea of taking care of you?'

'I'm just a bit damp,' I lied. 'I think I'll go straight upstairs and have a hot shower. Goodnight.'

I was half out of the door before he exclaimed, 'Wait a minute! I want to talk to you.'

'About what?' I asked, slowly turning to look

at him, my pulse beating heavily.

'About this.' He held out his hand. In the palm lay something so small that I had to go across the room before I could be sure what it was—my wedding ring.

'Oh, you found it!' I was pleased, but when I looked up and saw his face taut with fury a shudder ran through me. Why was he angry?

'When were you in my room?' he demanded.

'In your . . .' I stared at him incredulously, fighting a tickle at the back of my nose that was making my eyes water.

'Yes! In my room—right by the drawer where I keep some spare cash. There's five pounds missing. Aren't we giving you enough already?'

'But . . . Bev, I've never been in your room. Why would I . . .' I had to stop. A sneeze shook me, hurting my head. With one hand shading my stinging eyes, I looked up at him. 'That's an awful thing to say!'

'It was a lousy thing to do,' he raged. 'But it's typical of you. You're putting on a good act, but you really haven't changed at all. Oh, get out of my sight! You look like a drowned rat. Go and get dry. And take this with you.' Thrusting the ring into my hand, he stormed across to the record player.

'It's a lie!' I denied, sniffing. 'You're not being fair. I didn't take any money. I've never been in your room.'

'I don't intend to discuss it,' Bevis said coldly. 'Goodnight, Pamela.'

'Well, I'm not going to leave it at that! Wherever I lost this ring, it wasn't in your . . .'

My voice was drowned by the sudden blast of the 1812 Overture, guns, bells and all, turned up to top volume.

The room shook with it. Putting my hands over my ears, I ran for the door. The noise died down when I was half-way up the stairs, but I didn't go back. I had had quite enough for one night.

Despite a hot, soothing shower, my mind was in ferment as I lay waiting for sleep. It seemed ages before I drifted into oblivion. Then, somewhere in the middle of the night, I had a terrifying dream, as illogical as most dreams. I could never remember how it began, but it ended with me fleeing through a mirror maze, pursued by something unspeakable. Screaming, I blundered along, distorted images of myself looming up on all sides. Suddenly something grabbed me and I fought it desperately.

'Pamela!' The voice sent the dream flying in shreds back to the limbo from whence it had come. I found myself blinking against the light, staring up at Bevis, who was holding my shoulders and shaking me.

'Whatever's the matter?' Marjorie asked from the doorway where she stood bleary-eyed in her nightdress.

'Nothing, mother,' Bevis said shortly. 'She had a nightmare, that's all. Go back to bed before you catch cold.'

'Well, if you're sure ...' she muttered through a yawn, turning away.

My heart was beating much too fast, though the fear was leaving me. I took several deep breaths to calm myself.

'The same dream?' Bevis asked anxiously.

'What? Oh—no. Just a dream, this time.'

He laid a cold hand on my forehead. 'At least you're not feverish. I was afraid you'd caught a chill.'

'Afraid?' I said bitterly, remembering the way we had parted. 'Don't you mean you wished I had? First I'm a liar and now I'm a thief. Get out of my room!'

I turned over, pulling the blankets round my face, and felt beneath my cheek the hard shape of the book of quotations which I had left under the pillow. Bevis remained where he was, sitting on the bed in the pale blue pyjamas that made him look as vulnerable as a little boy. I hate, I love ... the words echoed through my mind, the whole verse etched indelibly. Sudden tears stung behind my tight-closed lids. I wished he would go away.

'I didn't mean it,' he said.

'Didn't mean what?' I asked in a sullen, muffled voice.

'What I said earlier. It's just so much easier to be angry with you. I'd worked myself up to it. I had to say it. But I don't believe it. Does that make sense?'

'No, it doesn't.'

Bevis heaved a long, slow sigh. 'I know it doesn't, but I can't explain it any better. Are you all right now?'

'I'm fine.'

'Then I'll let you get back to sleep. If you need me . . . Goodnight.'

I felt him touch my hair briefly before he left. The light clicked out and the door softly closed, leaving me crying into my pillow.

* * *

My step-brother had already gone out by the time I went down for breakfast.

'Gone for a walk,' Marjorie said. 'I don't think he slept very well, to tell you the truth. I've seen him before looking heavy-eyed and it usually means he's lost some sleep. How are you feeling this morning? No more dreams?'

'No, thank goodness. I'm sorry I woke you. Was I making a noise?'

'You screamed. I must confess it frightened me. For a minute I thought . . . But as long as it was only a dream . . . Pamela, did you see Lorraine yesterday?'

'Briefly, why?'

'She came to the cottage to help, as you had planned?'

'She did, but since there was no work in

155

progress she didn't stop long. James took her home.'

'I see,' Marjorie said thoughtfully. 'Oh, I'm sorry, I haven't asked you if you had a nice time last night.'

'Not really. James and I managed to fall out.'

'About Lorraine?'

'Lorraine?' I said in surprise. 'Good heavens, no.'

'But you did say James took her home yesterday, and not Bevis.' She frowned. 'He told me she was ill, you know. I didn't think it was the truth. Have they quarrelled? It's a shame. She's such a nice girl.'

'I don't know the first thing about it,' I told her, wishing I had been more discreet. But I remembered Lorraine saying in disgust, 'I was right yesterday, wasn't I? Wasn't I?'

Right about what? I wondered.

'I've known there was something wrong with Bevis ever since he came in on Friday night,' Marjorie was saying, shaking her head. 'He's been so irritable and restless. Perhaps he thinks I don't notice, but I know him too well. Still, they'll make it up, don't you think?'

'Yes, probably,' I said, since that was what she wanted to hear. 'Did Bevis say where he was going for his walk?'

'On to the moors, I think. At least, he went in that direction. Are you going to find him?'

'I thought I might.'

156

'Oh yes, do. Try to cheer him up, darling. I hate to see him looking so unhappy, but he won't talk to me. Perhaps he needs someone of his own generation. I'm going to church with Phyllis and Albert. Make yourselves some coffee if you want some.'

I was doubtful about my ability to 'cheer up' my stepbrother, but I wanted to see him, to talk the whole thing out. There must be some way we could live in peace, without tearing each other apart every time we met.

The earth was still wet from the previous night's rain, which had brought down a lot more leaves and made the path up through the woods treacherously slippy. I could see no sign of Bevis in the bare valley beyond, so carefully negotiated my way down the steep path to the stream. Here was the rock where I had been sitting when I first remembered that cliff-top meeting with a man whose name I now knew was Paul. But it was long ago and Paul, whoever he was, had gone from my life. The memory was of no use to me now.

To my left, the land climbed slowly into folded hills that looked less than inviting beneath the scudding grey clouds. Instead I turned right, following the stream. The shallow valley grew steeper as I walked towards a shoulder of the hill where the stream turned a bend. Beyond, the valley narrowed to a little gorge and the stream had cut into soft rock, leaving vertical banks on either side. The track I was following gradually climbed the hill, a series of bare patches worn into the grass. It was tricky walking, balancing on what few flat spaces the steep hill offered.

Pausing to get my breath, feeling dizzy from vertigo, I glanced ahead and saw Bevis about a hundred yards ahead of me, nearing the top of the hill. I cupped my hands to my mouth, teetering helplessly, and called his name.

I saw him jerk round, lose his balance. To my horror, he slipped on the narrow way. I could only stand and watch, appalled, as he slithered and rolled, fetching up with a sickening lurch that I felt myself, half across the bed of the stream.

No longer worried for my own safety, I hurried along the path and edged crabwise down the steep slope. Bevis was dragging himself out of the stream, his trousers soaked.

'Oh, Bev . . .'

He looked up at me, his face livid with pain and fury.

I backed away, frightened.

'Damn you, Pamela!' he said hoarsely. 'You did that deliberately. If I get my hands on you . . .'

He was on his feet, hands out, but when his weight came on his left ankle it buckled under him, sending him crashing to the ground. Only by an effort did I save him from rolling back into the stream.

He looked up at me, trying to say

158

something. He was pale as death. As I flung myself down beside him his eyes closed and he went completely limp.

CHAPTER EIGHT

Bevis's ankle was sprained. When he came round he let me examine it, but wouldn't allow me to remove his shoe, which he said he would need for walking.

'You can't walk!' I exclaimed.

'Of course I can. Help me up. I shall have to lean on you.'

In that way we slowly negotiated the valley and returned to the Hall, neither of us mentioning the accusation he had flung at me. I spoke only to encourage him, though by half way I was so tired myself that talking was too much of an effort. Bevis was no lightweight, even when he was only partly leaning on me.

As we reached the kitchen, I heard the doorbell ringing. It went on insistently as we moved into the Hall.

'You'd better answer it,' Bevis said breathlessly, flopping onto the bottom stair with relief.

The visitor was James, carrying a bunch of mixed flowers. 'Pamela, I . . .'

'Thank goodness!' I sighed. 'You're just the person we need. Bev's sprained his ankle. Can

159

you give me a hand to get him to bed?'

He came in, putting down the flowers on the hall table, looking at the weary Bevis with dislike.

'How did he do that?' he wanted to know.

'He fell. Out on the moors.' I mopped my wet brow tiredly. 'Please, James . . .'

With obvious reluctance, he helped me support Bevis up the stairs and along the corridor to his room, where my step-brother collapsed across the bed as though all his strength was gone. He looked so ill that I was frantic.

'Phone the doctor, will you?' I appealed to James. 'I must get him comfortable.'

He hesitated, glancing sideways at the prostrate Bevis. For the second time I was aware of his unwillingness to help a man he detested.

'James!'

'What's the doctor's name?'

'McCauley,' Bevis replied. 'He's in the book.'

James gave me a scowling glance. 'I'm doing this for you, not for him. I came here to talk to you.'

'Later,' I promised. 'And please hurry.'

Manhandling Bevis straight on the bed, I took off his shoes and socks. His left ankle was swollen alarmingly, turning blue, but the colour in his face was coming back. He watched me with a mocking light in his eyes, except when he winced.

'Why do you bother?' he asked at length. 'Didn't you hear what I said earlier?'

'You were raving,' I said shortly.

'Maybe I was. I can believe anything of you, until you're actually with me. How can you be two people?'

'How can *you*?' I returned.

'I only wish I knew. Perhaps if I understood it I could . . .'

With that, Marjorie rushed into the room, pale with worry. They had met James in the hall, she said. Phyllis was phoning the doctor.

'I'll live,' Bevis answered her anxious enquiries. 'I only turned my ankle, mother. I don't know what all the fuss is about.'

'He must be feeling better,' I remarked. 'He's being disagreeable already.'

But the badinage was for Marjorie's benefit. Inwardly I was hurting. Why should Bevis think that I wanted to hurt him?

That damned money again! I wondered if my father had realised how much trouble he was brewing for his family with that will.

Marjorie was questioning Bevis about what had happened, but this time he only said he had slipped.

'You're not fit to be let out alone!' she scolded. 'Oh, Pamela . . . James asked me to remind you that he's waiting to see you.'

I passed Phyllis on the stairs. She informed me that the doctor was on his way and that my 'young man' was waiting in the sitting-room.

He was gazing out of the window, but turned and put on a smile, bending to pick up the flowers which he had left on a chair.

'For you. I raided, my aunt's garden. I couldn't think of any other way of apologising, not on a Sunday, with all the shops shut.'

I took the flowers, thinking ungratefully that he wasn't very original with his offerings. 'Thank you, James.'

'I *am* sorry about last night,' he said. 'But any man would have been put-out, being called by someone else's name.'

'And by a woman who's drunk as an owl,' I said flatly, quoting his own words.

From his expression I guessed that he had expected me instantly to accept his apology and, probably, to melt sweetly into his arms. So he was a little taken-aback by my reply.

'I didn't mean that,' he assured me. 'I was angry. Darling, I've asked you to forgive me— for all of it.'

'And for today? For not wanting to help my brother?'

'Oh, come on, Pam! After what he did to me? After what he said?'

'And what about the things *you* said. You wanted him to hit you, didn't you? You thought it would turn me against him. You've been trying to do that since the first time I saw you. Why, James?'

His eyes narrowed. 'What I would like to

know is why you're defending him all of a sudden. Have you forgotten that he's the only one with reasons for wanting you out of the way?'

'Which is exactly what he told the police,' I informed him. 'It wasn't Bevis. It may not have been anyone. Perhaps it *was* just an accident. I don't want to hear you say another word about it, James.'

'So suddenly he's a paragon of virtue,' James sneered. 'That isn't the way you used to feel about him, Pamela. Will you still think he's so wonderful when you get your memory back? Just what is he to you?'

'He's my brother!'

'But he's not. He's not related in any way. If your father hadn't needed a substitute son . . .' He stopped himself.

'Go on, James. What were you going to say? If my father hadn't married Marjorie I'd be a rich woman now? Is that it? You know, you're excessively concerned about that money.'

He didn't reply for a while, just looked at me in growing fury. At last he burst out, 'It's him, isn't it? It's Bevis. You've realised that if you marry him you can still get your hands on the lot. That's what you're planning, isn't it?'

'For a man who professes to be in love with me,' I said coldly, 'you don't appear to have a very high opinion of my character.'

'You always were a mercenary little bitch. I should have known you wouldn't have changed much. There are other fish in the sea, you know.'

'Then go dangle your hook somewhere else!' I retorted.

Striding to the door, he collided with Phyllis, nearly knocking her over. He didn't bother to apologise. He carried straight on and slammed out of the house.

'Well!' Phyllis exclaimed. 'I was coming to ask if he was staying for lunch, but if you ask me it's a good job he isn't. I've never seen such bad manners in my life. And him an honourable, too.'

'An honourable what?' I asked.

'Honourable ... you know! The Hon. James. His father's a duke, or a lord, or something. Didn't you know? But it just goes to show not all of them are gentlemen ... By the way, the doctor's come.'

'Has he? That was quick.'

'Oh, he only lives half a mile away. Lunch will be about half an hour ... Have you found your ring yet?'

'My ring? Oh—yes, thank you. Bevis found it.'

'Did he? Where?'

'In the bathroom.' It was the first place that came into my head, 'Is there anything I can do to help with the lunch?'

'No thanks. It's all under control.' She gave me a funny, puzzled look, and came to relieve me of the flowers I was still holding. 'In the bathroom, you say?'

'Yes. I can't have searched very carefully. Why don't you put those flowers in your flat? We've got enough here, what with roses and chrysanths. That seems to be the extent of James's imagination.'

Frowning to herself, she went away, and only when she had gone did it occur to me to wonder at her interest in the ring. Why shouldn't it have been in the bathroom? Come to think of it, where *had* Bevis found it? Had it really been in his room?

Hearing Marjorie and the doctor coming down the stairs, I hurried into the hall to ask how Bevis was. His ankle was not broken, the doctor assured me, only badly sprained. He had given instructions for the patient to remain in bed for a couple of days, then slowly get back to his normal routine.

'Bevis is sleeping now,' Marjorie told me when the doctor had gone. 'He's really shaken up. It must have been a nasty fall.'

'It was,' I said. 'It's a mercy he didn't break his neck.'

'You were there?'

'Well, not actually with him, but I saw . . . I'm afraid it may have been my fault, Marjorie. The path's tricky there. I called to him, and when he looked round he lost his footing.'

'Oh, dear! But don't blame yourself, darling. It's just a patch of bad luck that we're going through. One thing after another lately.

165

I think I need a small sherry. Will you join me?'

*　　*　　*

Bevis slept for most of the afternoon. Marjorie kept going to check on him and coming back to say worriedly that he still didn't look well but the sleep would do him good after his restless night.

After one of these trips, I heard her using the phone, though I couldn't hear what she was saying, and then she went straight to the kitchen. Worried, in case she had thought it necessary to send for the doctor again, I went after her, intending to ask after Bevis, but as my fingers touched the kitchen door I heard words which made me stop.

'. . . and she said he hit James Summerton. James *did* have a cut on his lip. Did you notice?'

'I can't say I did,' Phyllis replied in a hard voice. 'But it doesn't surprise me. That step-daughter of yours is to blame. She's put a spell on Bevis, if you ask me. He's not been himself since she came into the house.'

'Pamela?' Marjorie said in horror. 'Oh, no!'

'Oh, yes! You're too nice yourself to see through her, but she doesn't fool me. She's been scheming ever since she came into the house. It wouldn't surprise me if Bevis wasn't right in the first place. Maybe she *is*

166

pretending, to get round you *and* him. Even James Summerton saw it in the end.'

'Saw what?' Marjorie asked breathlessly.

'What she's planning, being all sweetness and light, twisting you round her finger. I heard what he said to her, before he finally flung out in disgust—and who can blame him? It's the money she's after all right. If she can get her hooks into Bevis she'll end up with the lot, won't she? You said it yourself, Marjorie. She was against your marriage to her father. She never accepted it.'

'I can't believe . . .'

'I know you can't. You don't *want* to believe it, do you? You want everything to be lovely. But miracles don't happen, a leopard doesn't change its spots. James Summerton saw it; I saw it; and now you say Lorraine sees it, too. If you want to save your son from her clutches you'd better . . .'

Unable to take any more, I stepped through the door and confronted them, shocked by the spiteful, vicious allegations, and angry, too.

'Yes, I've been listening,' I admitted before either of them could speak. 'That's one more thing you can hold against me, Phyllis, but I gather you're not averse to a little eaves-dropping yourself, since you heard my conversation with James. But he was wrong, and you're wrong.' To my disgust and despair, I was on the verge of tears.

Marjorie looked pale and unhappy, out of

167

her depth, but Phyllis was made of sterner stuff. She squared her shoulders and looked me defiantly in the eye.

'You were the cause of Bev's quarrel with Lorraine, weren't you? Don't deny it!'

'I don't know *what* they quarrelled about,' I said, my voice thick.

'I just phoned Lorraine,' Marjorie said miserably. 'I thought a visit from her would help Bevis feel better. But she said . . . she said it was *you* I ought to be asking. Pamela . . . he didn't hit James, did he?'

'Yes, I'm afraid he did. But so would I have done, in his shoes. James was saying vile things'.

'Oh yes!' Phyllis crowed. 'Jealous of each other. Fighting over *you.*'

'That's not true!' I couldn't stop myself from bursting into tears. Sobbing, I turned and fled through the hall, up the stairs. There was only one thing to do. Leave. At once. Even the horrors of the cottage were preferable to living under suspicion at the Hall.

Throwing my case on to the bed, I began to fling my belongings into it. I could hardly see what I was doing, blinded by hot tears that coursed down my face without hindrance. In the back of my mind I was aware of Bevis calling me from his room, but I ignored him. I didn't want to see him. I didn't want to see anybody. I wanted to be left alone, to get back to the cottage where I belonged, whatever waited for me there.

The door behind me crashed open, making me be still.

'What the hell is going on?' Bevis demanded.

'You're supposed to be in bed!' I cried, and went on with my frantic packing until his hand fell on my arm and spun me round to face him. He was leaning on a walking stick, a sweater over his pyjamas.

'Leave me alone, Bevis!'

'I will not!' Letting the stick thud to the floor, he took hold of me with both hands. 'You'll tell me what's wrong.'

'I can't!'

'You can!'

I tried to jerk away, but only unbalanced him and flung out my arms to save him from falling. Then somehow we were holding each other tightly. I wept helplessly against him, loving him desperately and knowing I shouldn't.

'It's true, then,' Marjorie said sadly from the doorway.

Appalled, I stopped crying and drew away from Bevis as he looked round at his mother.

'What's true?' he growled.

She couldn't frame a reply, so I did, in a low, husky voice, 'That I'm plotting to entice you into marriage, solely to get my greedy hands on all my father's money. That's what Phyllis says, and James, and Lorraine . . .'

'Bloody rubbish!' Bevis snorted, leaning on my shoulder as he hopped to the bed and sat down heavily next to my untidily-packed suitcase. 'What the hell do they know about it? Is that why you're packing?'

'Yes, it is. And don't try to stop me. From now on I'll live my own life.'

'Where?'

'At the cottage.'

'Are you crazy?' he roared.

'I must have been, ever to hope I could repair the damage I've done. The wounds go too deep. None of you really trust me.'

With one sweep of his arm he pushed the case off the other side of the bed and, as I leaped to save it, fastened his hand round my arm and made me sit beside him.

'My wrist!' I gasped. 'Bev . . .'

'Be thankful it's not your neck,' he growled, but he lessened the pressure of his fingers. 'Now, mother, you sit down, too. We'll talk this out sensibly. What started it?'

'I telephoned Lorraine,' Marjorie said in a small voice, moving to a chair by the dressing-table. 'I thought she might come and . . .'

'And sweet little Lori told you I was carrying on with Pamela?' Bevis guessed. 'That's what she accused me of, but it's not true.'

'She didn't exactly say that,' Marjorie replied, chewing her lip unhappily. 'But she said I was calling the wrong girl. She sounded awfully bitter. And she said that you and

James . . .'

'Had a fight?' Bevis supplied. 'Yes, we did. And I'd do it again, given the same circumstances. What of it?'

'Bevis!' She looked at him in alarm. 'It's not funny.'

'Who's laughing? So what happened then?'

'I . . . went to ask Phyllis what she thought, and she said . . .' She recounted the conversation I had heard, and the way I had burst in, ending, 'It wasn't a very pleasant scene, Bevis.'

'I'm sure it wasn't,' he agreed drily. 'But then your friend Phyllis isn't a very pleasant woman when she's roused.'

Outraged, Marjorie got to her feet. 'I won't hear a word against Phyllis. She's been a very good friend to me.'

'And you've been very good to her, mother, more than generous. I haven't said anything before because I knew it made you happy to help an old friend, but do you realise that your confidante is the biggest gossip around? Our private business is discussed all over Butterford and Cannonfield because Phyllis can't keep anything to herself. And I know for a fact that she's tried to make trouble between us and Pamela.'

'Bevis! How can you?'

'It's time I put my spoke in. She's gone over the top this time. I found Pamela's wedding ring—in my room.'

Eyes round with astonishment, Marjorie sat down again. 'What has that to do with Phyllis?'

'I'm as sure as dammit that she planted it there, near the drawer where there's five pounds missing from my extra cash. I thought at first that Pamela had ... But she couldn't have known there was money there to take. It puzzled me, until Phyllis was in my room earlier and obviously looking to see if the ring was still there.'

'Why should she do such a thing?' Marjorie demanded, still defending her friend. 'She doesn't need money.'

'She didn't do it for the money! She did it to make trouble. You were getting too friendly with Pamela and Phyllis found herself relegated to the background, so she thought she'd try to put Pamela out of favour. But don't take my word for it. Ask her.'

Marjorie blanched. 'I couldn't.'

'That's up to you. Maybe it would be better to let it lie. But just remember that Phyllis is capable of being extremely vindictive when it suits her.'

Marjorie was clearly shaken by the revelations, but said stoutly, 'I'll give you the five pounds, Bevis. I'm sure Phyllis wouldn't mean any real harm. It's my fault if she's felt neglected. Poor Phyllis. I'll go and tell her everything's all right again.'

We were silent when she had gone. Bevis slowly unwrapped his hand from around my wrist and sat with his head bent, thinking. For myself, I felt numb, drained, miserable.

'I admire her optimism,' he said eventually. 'Everything's not all right, is it?'

'No,' I agreed in a low voice. 'Far from it, if you seriously think I deliberately sprained your ankle.

He turned to look at me. 'That's not what I meant.'

'It's what you *said*.'

'I was angry, and in pain. I told you how it is. For some reason I grab at every chance to detest you, but it never lasts . . . What did you think of Catullus?'

'I've read better,' I said swiftly, jumping to my feet. That was much too dangerous a subject. 'You're supposed to be in bed, you know. I don't want to have to pick you off the floor again. You're very heavy.' Stooping down, I picked up the walking stick and held it out to him. 'Can you manage, or do you want some help?'

He lifted his gaze slowly from the stick to my face, then glanced behind me at the door, where Marjorie had reappeared.

'I quite forgot to tell you,' she said. 'What with Bevis hurting his ankle and then all this bother . . . You had a visitor this morning, Pamela, just as we were leaving for church.'

'*I* did?' I exclaimed. 'Who?'

'Alan somebody. He said . . .'

'Alan Hart?' Bevis asked in surprise,

glancing up at me.

'Yes, that's right. He's been using Pamela's garden, so he said. Do you know about that?'

'We met him yesterday,' Bevis said. 'What did he want, mother?'

'He brought the final month's rent. Four pounds. Here it is.'

Bemused, I hooked the walking stick over my arm and took the notes from her. 'I didn't realise he paid rent. Thank you, Marjorie.'

'That's all right, darling. I'm sorry I didn't give it to you before now, but it went clean out of my head. And that's odd, because all through the service this morning I was thinking about something else he said. But of course when we came home and found Bevis hurt, everything else went by the board.'

'What "else" did he say?' Bevis wanted to know.

'Nothing that matters, really. I can't think what made him ... He particularly wanted to see Pamela, but she'd gone out looking for you and he couldn't wait. Then he asked me if I was sure she *was* Pamela, and I said *of course* we were sure. Well, who else could she be? But it was a funny thing to say, wasn't it?'

'Hilarious,' Bevis said. His tone should have been dry but it sounded more thoughtful and he glanced at me again, speculatively.

Feeling chilled, I said swiftly, 'He probably couldn't believe that I didn't recognise him. If we were ...' I stopped, remembering that

Marjorie didn't know what we suspected about my relationship with Alan Hart.

'That's what *I* thought at the time,' Bevis said. 'He did stare at you pretty obviously. Mother, did he explain why he had doubts?'

'I didn't ask him,' Marjorie said severely. 'There *is* no doubt. I wish I'd never told you, Bevis, if you're going to hold an inquest. Alan Hart can't possibly know Pamela better than we do. It's too silly for words. We *know* her. I refuse to discuss it any more.'

'Why?' Bevis asked.

'Because there *is* nothing to discuss!' Marjorie was upset, her hands fluttering aimlessly. 'Do you think I don't know my own step-daughter?'

'You said yourself she doesn't look any older.'

'Why should she? Anyway, with her hair cut short it makes her look younger. I saw her before she had it cut, you know.'

'She's slimmer, too.'

'Because she hasn't been eating properly!' Marjorie exclaimed.

'Her voice is different, as well. Huskier.'

'The smoke caused that! They told me in hospital. Bevis ... I don't know what you're trying to do, but I wish you'd stop. She *is* Pamela. We know she is. Just because one man who hardly knows her was stupid enough to say ... Oh, I won't listen to any more.' And she hurried away.

Throughout the exchange I had stood silent, amazed. Of course I was Pamela Lane. There was no question about it.

'One man who hardly knows you?' Bevis softly repeated his mother's words. 'Or one man who has known you very well, and recently—more recently than we have.'

'One man who is mistaken,' I said flatly. 'I know who I am.'

'You only know what we've told you,' Bevis pointed out. 'Is there one single thing you actually remember?'

'Two things, I remember a man called Paul, who hurt me once. And I remember the living-room of the cottage, as it used to be. There were flowers painted on the chimney breast, weren't there, and a woven rug covering the couch?'

'There may have been. I wouldn't know.'

Saddened, I handed him the walking stick and went to put the four pound notes in my handbag. 'You don't want to believe I'm myself, do you, Bev? If I were someone else, you could forget about the past. There would be no past for us.'

'Maybe that's so,' he said in a soft, sad voice. 'On the other hand, mother is only too anxious for you to be Pamela come back. It's been the dream of her life these past five years. She's not going to look too closely now that the miracle's happened. We believe what we want to believe, most of the time. But she must have thought about it. She answered without hesitation—as though she had it all figured out.'

'Her answers are the right answers, Bev.' I turned to him, leaning on the dressing-table. 'You *do* know me, don't you?'

'I think I do. But it's easy for people to deceive themselves. We must talk to Alan Hart.'

'Why?' I asked desperately.

'If he was your lover, he'll know you better than anyone.'

'*If* he was!'

'That's what we have to find out.'

'Oh, Bev . . .' Tears had got into my voice, tears of fright. 'Do you know what you're saying? If I wasn't myself . . . Who can I be? Must I be nobody again? We *know* who I am. I'm Pamela Lane, your step-sister. I've made mistakes in the past, but now I'm trying to rectify that. Isn't that enough? Must you question it? Why should we risk making trouble for Alan Hart? Whatever there was between us—if there was anything at all—it's all over. Don't let's rake it up again. I *am* Pamela! Believe it!'

Sighing, he got to his feet, leaning heavily on the stick. 'I do believe it. That's the hell of it. There's no logical alternative, is there? I only wish there was. I had got over you completely. I despised what you were. And now . . .'

'Don't, Bev,' I begged. 'Please don't.'

'But you see how it is? I don't want to care about you, but I do, and I hate you for making me care when I ought to know better. I love what you seem to be, but I hate what you used to be, and I'm afraid you might go back to being that way. I know just how Catullus must have felt when he wrote that poem. "In agony" describes it exactly.'

'Stop it!' I fled past him, across the room to the window, clutching the curtain in one hand while the other was pressed hard against my mouth. Controlling myself with difficulty, I said raggedly, 'Remember the bad things, Bev. Think the worst. There's no point in anything else.'

'That's what I keep telling myself,' he said sadly. 'But it doesn't make the slightest difference . . . I'm cold. I'll get back to bed.'

Common humanity made me turn to ask, 'Can you manage?'

'I'd better, don't you think?' Bevis replied, his eyes holding mine. 'I've already made enough of a fool of myself for one day. If you come near me again . . .'

Swallowing hard, my heart beating erratically, I swung back to the window, staring unseeingly at the view until I heard him reach his own room. For the first time in days I found myself trying to remember what had happened before this last twelve days. If only I could feel again as I had felt then. If only I

178

knew what had made me behave as I had done.

But the barrier was still there, with only the chink that showed me a cliff-top and a man named Paul telling me he was going to marry someone else. Why was that the only memory I could dredge up? Why didn't I remember my husband, or James, or Bevis? Why Paul, who was long gone from my life?

It was so infuriating.

*   *   *

Before I went to bed that night I repacked my case—carefully, this time. It was no longer a matter of emotional impulse, but a calm, logical decision. I had brought nothing but trouble to Butterford Hall. No good could come of my staying. Whatever dangers waited for me at the cottage—if any—they were of my own making. I had no right to bring them to the Hall.

My problems, too, were for me to solve. I must begin sewing again. My fingers would remember how to make gingham mice once I applied myself to the task, and there were other ways of earning money, plus the possibility of Social Security. They might at least pay my rent until I had my affairs in some sort of order, by which time I might have recovered from my amnesia.

If there ever had been a threat to my life, it

no longer worried me. Whilst I had no death-wish, neither had I any burning desire to go on living. My life had been one long disaster and if someone chose to end it that was fine by me, or so I assured myself. It would also, in the long run, relieve Marjorie and Bevis from any feeling of responsibility for me, so it was a chance I was fully prepared to take.

I lay awake for a long time re-thinking my reasons for leaving and finding them sound. It was the sensible thing to do, I was sure.

CHAPTER NINE

Unfortunately, Marjorie didn't feel the same way about it when I told her at breakfast, calmly and reasonably, that I had changed my mind about staying at the Hall.

'But the trouble hasn't been *your* fault, darling,' she said worriedly.

'None of it would have happened if I hadn't come here. Because of me, you're at odds with Phyllis, you're worrying and ... I'm hurting Bevis, Marjorie. That's the last thing I want to do. I'll keep in touch this time, though. We'll still be friends—and not because of any clause in that will my father left. I'll call in occasionally and let you know how I'm getting along. I'll really feel better if I can sort things out myself.'

180

'You mean you won't feel beholden to us. You always were too proud, Pamela. But Bevis isn't going to like this, you know.'

'It's my decision, not his. Don't tell him until you have to. Say I've gone out for the day. It will be almost the truth.'

'Aren't you going to see him before you go?'

'I think not. And please make sure that Phyllis doesn't tell him, either, not for a while. For his sake. You know what he's like. He's liable to try coming after me, and he shouldn't be using that ankle yet. When you have to tell him, say that I know what I'm doing and that I'll be glad to see him when he's better, but for now I want to get settled in in peace.'

Going upstairs to fetch my case, I moved quietly, but not quietly enough. Bevis called me from his room.

'Good morning,' I called through the door. 'How are you?'

'Come and see,' he invited.

'Not now, Bev. I'm busy. See you later.' And I escaped without further comment.

Outside on the drive, Marjorie was waiting in her car, with a basketful of food to 'keep me going'.

'You shouldn't have bothered,' I said.

'It's the least I can do. You don't seem to realise, Pamela, it gives me pleasure to give you things. And while we're on the subject you don't owe me anything. What little I've done I've been happy to do. No, don't argue. This

181

time I'm putting my foot down. You will start with a clean sheet. On the way we'll call in at the shop and the garage and pay what you owe, and then you can forget about the past and work on the future.'

And that was what we did, though I took mental note of the sums involved and promised myself to present her with a cheque for the full amount she had given me some day when I had enough savings.

When we reached the cottage she came in with me and I made some coffee for us both.

'What are you going to do about this room?' she asked, staring at the mess the fire had left.

'Clean it up,' I replied, swallowing the fear that had come into my throat the moment I stepped through the back door. At all costs, I must hide it from Marjorie. 'I can do it myself. The carpet from the bedroom will go in there, I think. The floorboards will hold for a while.'

'Phyllis and I will come and give you a hand.'

'No, Marjorie! You've already done too much.'

'Well, we'll see. You'll have to learn to receive gracefully, Pamela. Now, are you sure you'll be all right? You can still change your mind.'

'Don't worry about me. If I'm desperate I can always phone, or ride over on my bike. It's not that far. Come and have this coffee.'

I hoped I sounded convincing.

When Marjorie left, I stood at the gate watching her car go down the lane. As had happened the first time I came here, with Bevis, I was aware only of the loneliness of the place. A cold wind sighed through the trees that surrounded the cottage, bringing a constant flutter of dying leaves. Today there was no sunshine, no birdsong, only heavy grey clouds and that wind. Shivering, I went back into the cottage.

The cats, too, had deserted me, it seemed. It would have been pleasant to have even their disinterested company. But it was no good brooding. Here I had come and here I would stay. Work was what I needed.

Shutting my mind against the fear that threatened to stifle me, I lit a fire in the living-room grate, then began to clear the blackened debris. When that was done I rescued the bucket which still lay on the front path where I had fallen over it, filled it with hot soapy water and began the scrubbing-up operations.

I was so determined to make a change in that room whose memories haunted me that I forgot about time and food, everything but the job I was engaged in, until a sound from outside filtered through to me and I glanced at my watch.

It was a quarter to three. A car was coming up the lane.

I heard it stop outside. I went to the window, soap and filth up to my elbows, my pulse beating fast. Beyond the shrubs I could just see the roof of a white car. Bevis! Oh, no, he mustn't come.

There was no sign of anyone leaving the car. The horn tooted sharply twice, as if summoning me. Of course, he couldn't walk. It was a wonder he had been able to drive. I could imagine the scene there must have been at the Hall, Marjorie protesting and her son being stubborn.

Going into the kitchen, I dried my hands and hastily tidied my hair, though it was blown untidy again the moment I went outside. I hurried down the path, opened the gate ... and only then did I see that it wasn't Bevis's Viva but another car, standing there with its engine running and its boot open.

There was no one in the car.

Puzzled, I stood by the open boot and looked along the track that led into the woods. Had someone come to dump something, or collect something?

A *white* car! Belatedly I realised the possible significance of it. In the same moment there was a movement behind me. I whirled ... and that's all I remember.

*   *   *

Cold water shocked me awake. I was doused in it, drowning in it. I got a mouthful and noseful before I realised what was happening. The last

184

gasp of breath in my lungs cleared my nostrils as I kicked upwards. A pale pink sky opened above me. Floundering, I gulped in the clean fresh air and let out a wordless shout before slipping under again. Vaguely I was aware of a dog barking.

I was still half unconscious when my lashing hands encountered something stiff. A stick! I clung to it, pushing for the surface again, and the stick began to pull me along. My head came clear of the water. Through my choking and spluttering I saw a black figure outlined against the sky, looming over me as it extended a hand.

'Take it easy,' a male voice soothed. 'Easy. Shut up, Bess!'

The dog fell silent. I found myself half scrambling, half being pulled, on to a muddy slope, where I lay on my side gasping like a stranded fish. The dog snuffed round me until the man shooed her away. Slowly I became aware that I was almost naked, shivering in the cold air of dusk.

'You've banged your head, looks like,' the man said. 'Here, take my jacket. Can you walk? My house isn't far.'

At the time I didn't even bother to wonder what had happened. It took all my strength to stumble along clutching the man's supporting arm. I was chilled to the bone, shivering uncontrollably, my stockinged feet finding every stone and twig. To our right a lake glimmered in the last fading light of day and ahead of us there was a gate which the man opened.

I was limping as he led me along an asphalt road. All I wanted was to get warm and dry, to feel better. My head hurt abominably and I felt sick. Then we came to a neat white house with a neat white fence. I couldn't think, except about how awful I felt.

We came into the house, climbed some stairs. He switched on a light that was painfully brilliant to my sore eyes, but as I blinked and rubbed them I saw a bathroom, tiled all in blue.

'Take your time,' the man said. 'There's no rush.'

Before he left he turned on the taps. Steaming hot water gushed into the blue bath, filling the room with a mist of condensation. With cold, stiff arms, shudders running through me, I stripped off what little I was wearing—bra, pants and tights, and gingerly stepped into the hot water, slowly letting myself down until I was immersed. The bliss of that bath! It warmed me, soothed my hurts, made my cut feet ache and my aching head spin. What had happened? What had happened? But thinking only made my head hurt unbearably. I relaxed, and almost went to sleep.

Forcing myself awake, I climbed with aching limbs from the bath and wrapped myself in a clean, fluffy towel. I squinted with stinging eyes at my reflection in the mirror of a little cabinet on the wall, examining the lump above my temple that still bled freely.

And then I noticed my hair. It was cut short! Bewildered, frightened, I held up a short, wet lock. Who had cut it? And when? Was I dreaming? Was I mad?

Without preliminaries, my host walked into the bathroom, bringing a nightdress and negligee which he draped over a low stool.

'I found these. I suppose they're yours.'

'Yes, they are. Where did you find them?'

'Where you left them. In your car. Get dressed now I've made some supper. Come down when you're ready.'

My car? I thought in bewilderment. My car was here? How?

Still shaking, not from cold now, but from reaction and weakness, I dried myself and put on the clothes he had brought. On wobbly legs I made my way down the stairs. A big grandfather clock in the hall slowly beat time. It was just after eight.

A black and white collie came eagerly from the room to my right, woofing a greeting before letting me pat her head and fondle her ears.

'In here,' the man called.

It was a small room filled with old furniture, but it was clean and well-dusted. Pieces of porcelain stood on a sideboard, with a large

187

photograph of a smiling young woman dressed in a version of the New Look of the forties. In front of the electric fire a small table was laid for two and the man was ladling stew from a saucepan.

'I'm no cook, but it's all good stuff,' he told me, looking up and catching me glancing again at the photograph. 'My wife,' he told me. 'Sit down. Tuck in. I don't believe in ceremony.'

Again I obeyed. It was easier. The stew was plain but very palatable. We ate in silence, the dog lying in front of the fire with its nose on its paws, eyes fixed on its master.

He was a thick-set man with large, rough hands and unkempt grey hair. His face was ruddy, as though he worked a lot in the open. He wore corduroy trousers and a navy-blue sweater that needed washing and I judged him to be somewhere between fifty and sixty, though it was hard to tell. He didn't look at me once.

'What is this place?' I asked eventually, beginning to feel more human.

'My house.'

'I mean ... where are we? Is it near Butterford?'

'Miles away. Doon's the nearest village, if you can call it that. You were in the Doon reservoir. I suppose you didn't care what it was called, as long as it was deep enough.'

'Deep enough?' I queried.

'For your purposes. I'm not asking

questions. I don't want to know. I live my life and let people live theirs. Tonight you can stay here, but tomorrow if you want to go off and drown yourself I won't stop you.'

I felt sweat break out on my face and hands. 'Is that what I was doing?'

'What else would you call it?' He looked up at me then, his eyes sharp and watchful.

'I don't know. I've no idea how I got here. I was in Butterford, the last I remember, going to visit someone. The next thing I knew, I was drowning. You said my car is here?'

'By the water. And your clothes and shoes. By rights I should call the police, but I don't like to get involved. I like my privacy. If you've finished eating I'll show you your room. You can make up your own bed. I like to go to bed early.'

From the window of the room he gave me I could see out across the lake. A three-quarter moon was rising over the hills, glowing palely on the ruled water, and in the stillness I went over what had happened.

Plymouth, my flat, the bank. Paul, shame-facedly telling me that he had found someone else, telling me there on the cliff-top where I had been waiting for him so happily. I recalled the hurt that had made me resign my job at the bank where Paul was under-manager, and the way I had run home to mother, who was too busy running her two boutiques to provide the comfort and company I needed.

So I had decided to put it all behind me and go on a touring holiday, seeing some of the places I had always promised myself to visit some day. On the way north, speeding up the M4 to Scotland, I had realised that, after all, Paul wasn't worth breaking my heart over. From then on I had enjoyed the freedom that being uncommitted had brought me.

After a few days spent in Scotland, I came slowly south again, moving in easy stages through the Lake District, visiting Blackpool—which even in September was too crowded and commercial for my taste—exploring North Wales and its hidden valleys, moving across Cheshire towards the Peak District where my second cousin Pamela Lane lived. I had never seen her, but she sent regular Christmas cards to mother, who had often said she wished we could get to know Pamela. On impulse, I consulted my address book and my map and headed for Butterford. I remembered the village very clearly. And then ... then I had found myself drowning in the lake. What had happened to the rest of that day?

My host, whose name I never learned, had brought my suitcase and handbag to my room, so that in the morning I dressed warmly in my flame-coloured trouser suit. I brushed my hair carefully around the scab that had formed on my head, and was disturbed again by the style. I didn't remember having it cut. Yesterday it had been below my shoulders. Now it was cut short, in a side-swept fringe with soft wings either side of the face.

Troubled, I studied my hands. There were healing scratches all over them. Had that happened when I fell in the water?

Knowing that there were a lot of questions to be answered, I went downstairs. The house was quiet, but I found the kitchen, which was as clean and tidy as the rest of the house. The table was spread with a yellow cloth on which stood a dish and spoon, cup and saucer, and a note which said, 'Porridge on the stove. Coffee in the pot'. He was a man of few words.

I ached all over, particularly in my head. When I bent down the pain was so intense that I nearly passed out, so I moved carefully, keeping my head balanced as though it might fall off. It took me a long time to have breakfast.

There was still no sign of my host when I had washed my few dishes. I had slept late. It was almost eleven o'clock. I ventured out into the garden, which was as tidy as the house, autumn flowers growing in regimented clumps. Perhaps the man was retired, and spent all his time in his house and garden.

Hearing a car draw up with a grinding of gears, I went to the corner of the house. Beyond the white fence, the man was climbing out of my white Capri. His dog ran ahead of him, wagging her tail as she stopped before me, and I bent carefully to pet her.

'Had your breakfast?' the man asked.

I straightened, fighting a wave of dizziness that soon passed. 'Yes, thank you.'

'You'll want to be off, then. Where's your case?'

'Still upstairs, but it's packed. I wasn't sure . . .'

Without another word he went into the house. The dog followed me as I walked slowly to look at my car. There were scratches all along the bodywork, not deep, but noticeable. They had not been there yesterday. The keys were still in the ignition, where they must have been all night. It was an inexplicable puzzle.

Returning with my case, the man stowed it in the boot.

'Off you go, then. I can't wait about. I'm busy. Come on, Bess.'

'Thank you,' I called as he and the dog departed, but he didn't glance round. Obviously he didn't want my gratitude. He just wanted to be rid of an unwelcome intruder.

Climbing into the car, I took the maps from the glove compartment and tried to figure out where I was. The Doon reservoir lay in the heart of the Peak District, some twenty-odd miles from Butterford. Could I have driven all that way in a trance?

I remembered suddenly that I had been due to spend two nights at the Xanadu Motel. I had telephoned and booked a room for Wednesday and Thursday. In my handbag I had a note of the Motel's address, near Cannonfield. A main road would take me straight there.

First I had to negotiate the narrow lanes that dipped and climbed amid the wild grandeur of the Pennines. I took it slowly, my head hurting so much that at times I could hardly see. In several places the road was dangerous, deep valleys cutting sharply away with no fence for protection. It was with relief that I gained the relatively wide B road which would take me to Cannonfield. All my concentration was required for driving. When I reached the Motel I could stop and think.

The receptionist looked at me askance, her eyes flicking over my pale face and widening as she saw the contusion which my hair didn't properly conceal.

'Miss Forrester? I'm sorry, I have no record of a booking in that name. Yesterday and today, you said?'

'Yes.' I leaned on the counter, feeling giddy, hoping I wasn't going to make a fool of myself. 'I telephoned on Tuesday, but I couldn't make it yesterday.'

She was looking through her book, frowning. 'Someone may have made a mistake. You're sure it was for this week?'

'Oh, yes. At least . . . I think so. Wednesday and Thursday, the twenty-first and twenty-second.'

She gaped at me, then quickly recovered her

professional poise and turned back a page or two. 'Oh yes. That's right. You were here those two nights. You must be confused, Miss Forrester.'

'I was here? But . . .' I could feel my senses slipping and gripped the counter hard to stop them. 'What day is it now?'

'Tuesday. Tuesday the fourth of October. Do you want a room for tonight?'

I grasped at the chance of normalcy. 'Yes, please. I'm sorry. Stupid of me.'

'Are you sure you're feeling well?' she asked.

'Yes, I'll be all right. I had a bit of an accident, as you can see. My memory's playing tricks on me.'

I don't know how I got through the next few minutes until I was left alone in a warm room with a single bed on which I lay in relief, closing my eyes against the sight of the walls ballooning and shrinking. I hadn't lost a few hours. I had lost nearly two weeks.

I fell asleep, waking around four in the afternoon. Feeling better for the rest, I resolved to go back to Butterford to see if Pamela could throw any light on what had happened. I knew I had been on my way to visit her, and now I knew also that I had spent that night and the next here at the Xanadu Motel, but what had happened to the rest of the time?

Having taken a warm shower, I searched my

case for the royal blue skirt and jacket I had bought from mother's boutique just before leaving Dorset for my holiday. It wasn't there. That was another puzzle. I was sure I had been wearing it when I went to see Pamela.

I took my time over having a meal. I wasn't very hungry, though I hadn't eaten since I had breakfasted at the house of that strange man who rescued me from drowning. My head still ached dully.

The sun was going down in a glory of golden clouds as I drove down into the Butterford valley. A gateway among woods to my left seemed strangely familiar, but I couldn't place why, so I drove on, coming at last into the village which I remembered clearly. Too clearly. I knew that the man at the garage had a front tooth missing, though I didn't recall stopping for petrol, And the woman in the village shop had awful yellow hair. Without having to think about it, I turned like a homing pigeon into the gloomy Wood End Lane, where the light from the sunset was filtered by the tall trees.

And I remembered.

I slammed on my brakes and sat there, trembling, knowing now where I had been those two weeks, knowing what had happened to my blue suit. If I went to the cottage now, what would I find?

CHAPTER TEN

After a few minutes of furious thinking, I backed the car a few yards and turned off to the right. There was an almost-hidden track which I had subconsciously noticed every time I came down the lane. Tall bushes grew close on either side, their branches scraping along the car. The Capri had been this way before. *That* was how those marks came to be on its paintwork.

I couldn't get far. A tangle of bushes and trees barred my way. But when I climbed out of the car I realised that it would be completely hidden from the road.

Far above, beyond the shadowing branches of the trees, the sky was changing from gold to washed-out blue, but there was still enough light in the woods for me to see the faint track that someone had trodden through the undergrowth, little more than a way of flattened grass and bent branches. It led in the general direction of the cottage.

Locking the car, I followed that vague path. It veered and twisted, avoiding blackberry thorns and big roots, going round trees. And then, ahead of me, I glimpsed the roof of the cottage. A short distance further and I could see the back of the cottage, the rickety fence, the leaning sheds. A thread of smoke came from the chimney.

Here I found the place, a snug nest between two tree-roots, where someone had sat, flattening an areas of grass. I sat there myself, discovering a collection of sweet wrappers tucked under one of the roots. By leaning on the root and peering through the leaves of a hazel bush, I could still see the yard behind the cottage. Pale evening light glimmered on the windows I myself had washed.

I clearly heard the click of the back door latch. My second cousin, Pamela Lane, emerged into the yard, calling, 'Puss, puss, puss.' She was wearing a smock blouse, and a pair of blue jeans that were tighter on her than they had been on me. She had also had her hair cut like mine. We were almost doubles. Almost. She was four years older, an inch taller, weighing a little more. I remembered grimly how we had compared these points in astonishment, and how she had asked me all about myself—before she hit me over the head.

'There now,' she was crooning to the cats in a nasal voice. 'Isn't that lovely? Mummy's home now. Mummy will take care of you.' It sounded as though she had a cold.

I crouched there stupefied, wondering what on earth I should do next, when I heard a car cruising down the lane. It stopped outside the cottage with an audible rattle. Pamela had a visitor.

Fascinated, I saw her rush back into the cottage and close the door. A moment later, two men walked round the corner into the yard. Alan Hart—and Bevis, using his walking stick.

I stifled a sob of hope and fear. Bevis was no more than twenty feet from me as he knocked on the door in the growing dusk. But I stayed where I was, almost afraid to show myself, wondering how Pamela would deal with this.

She opened the door only a few inches. Her voice was low, but it carried clearly on the still air. 'I shouldn't come in, Bevis. I've got a frightful cold.'

'I brought Alan,' Bevis said. 'I phoned him, as I said I would. Will you let him talk to you?'

'What about?'

'You know what about. We discussed it. Don't be afraid.'

'I'm not afraid!' Her voice was suddenly acid, but she caught it and went on, 'I'm sorry. I'm not feeling very good. On top of this cold . . . My memory's come back. I remember everything up to the fire starting, but everything afterwards is a bit hazy. I don't remember us discussing Alan.'

Alan Hart stepped forward, asking, 'It *was* an accident, was it?'

'Yes, it was. I left the room. When I came back a log had fallen off the fire. The rug was blazing. I panicked, tripped over . . . Look, I'm really feeling lousy. I was just going to bed.

198

Can't it wait?'

Through the gathering dusk, in which the men couldn't possibly see Pamela clearly, I saw Alan Hart put his hand on the door to prevent her from closing it. 'Just tell me one thing—are you still planning to tell my wife what was going on between us?'

'Why should I bother?' Pamela, asked bitterly. 'Don't worry, Alan. Go back to your fat wife and forget about me. Bevis ... tell your mother I'll be round to see her when my cold's better.' And she closed the door.

The two men were little more than darker shadows now. They turned from the door.

'Well?' Bevis asked. 'What do you think?'

'I couldn't see very well, but from what she said ... It's Pamela, all right. It couldn't be anybody else.'

'It's what I was afraid of,' Bevis replied dully, as they disappeared from view round the corner of the cottage. He added something about memory and personality, but I couldn't catch what it was.

A light clicked on in the kitchen, shafting out into the yard. I saw a hand pull the curtain and was suddenly aware of a cold dampness rising from the ground beneath me.

Blundering through the dimness, I stumbled my way back towards where I had left the car, my hands up to protect my head. But I had waited too long. Beneath the trees it was already full dark. I couldn't see more than a foot, though above me the last faint glow of daylight still streaked the sky. I had to feel my way, inch by inch, not worrying too much about the brambles and nettles that scratched and stung my legs, as long as I didn't fall and jar my head, or bang it on a low branch. I must have gone astray. I seemed to have been ages in that dark wood, straining my eyes against the gloom, before I glimpsed to my right a paler piece of darkness which at last resolved itself into my car.

Thankfully, I climbed into the car. There was only one thing to do. I must go to the Hall. I didn't dare face Pamela alone and I didn't feel well enough to answer a lot of questions in a police station. The Hall it had to be, for I must tell someone what had happened. I could hardly drive away and leave the situation.

There were no cars on the driveway at the Hall. I wondered if Bevis had taken Alan Hart home after their visit to Pamela. Still, I could talk to Marjorie, and wait for Bevis in comfort. Wishing that I felt fit enough to face the coming scenes, I rang the doorbell.

It was Phyllis who answered, sour-faced when she saw me. 'What are you ringing for? You could have saved my legs. Well, come on in. They're in the sitting-room.'

'Both of them?' I asked.

'Naturally,' she said as she stumped away.

Since it seemed stupid to knock, though that was what I felt like doing, as a stranger, I opened the sitting-room door and went in. Bevis stared at me from his chair, speechless with surprise, while Marjorie jumped up and came to me. From her diffident manner, I guessed that Bevis had told her 'Pamela' was back to her sour self.

'My dear . . . You don't look at all well. Did you cycle over, with a bad cold? Is something wrong? Come and sit down.'

Now that I was with them, my legs felt weak. How lovely it had been to be welcomed here, to be cared for. I allowed myself just a few more minutes to luxuriate in it.

With a sigh of relief, I sat down in a corner of the comfortable settee, chancing a glance at Bevis, who was watching me with a frown between his brows, as if he knew that something was haywire but couldn't put his finger on the cause. That would make my task easier.

'Would you like a drink, or some coffee?' Marjorie asked.

'No, thank you. Nothing. I want to talk to you. Both of you.'

'Well, of course you can! You know that.' She sat down in the chair opposite Bevis. 'That's a new dress, isn't it? Have you been into Cannonfield? Oh, Pamela . . .'

'I'm not Pamela,' I said flatly, and let the silence lengthen. Marjorie just stared at me, but Bevis came out of his chair and stood by the hearth, favouring his left ankle.

'I do look like Pamela,' I admitted, 'and I *was* found unconscious in her cottage, so it was a natural mistake for you to make. I believed it, too, until yesterday. There didn't seem any other explanation. We talked about it, if you remember.' Again I glanced up at Bevis, who nodded.

'We believe what we want to believe,' he repeated his own words.

'Apparently that's so,' I agreed, turning back to Marjorie. 'Under the circumstances, what else could you believe? But I'm afraid I'm *not* Pamela Lane. I'm Susan Forrester.'

Marjorie licked her lips. 'But ... you have been here? It *was* you who ...'

'It was me you took such good care of, Marjorie, yes. I shall never be able to thank you enough. But despite what we all thought, I'm not your step-daughter.'

'Then who are you?' Bevis asked.

'My name is Susan Forrester,' I repeated. 'I'm twenty-four, and I live in Plymouth. I'm Pamela's second cousin. You see, my mother and Pamela's mother were cousins, and very close when they were young. After the first Mrs. Ennis died, my mother kept in touch with Pamela, through Christmas cards. We always said we must try to meet Pamela, but it never happened until two weeks ago.' I paused for comment, but they both seemed too stunned to speak, so I went on, 'I was on a touring holiday, and found myself practically passing

202

Pamela's door, so I decided to call on her. We were amazed to see how alike we were. She gave me a cup of tea and asked me all about myself. I told her a good deal, as I recall, how I had given up my job and was thinking of leaving Plymouth. She left the room for some reason and I sat there watching the fire, thinking how pleasant it was when there was a storm brewing outside, and . . .'

'She knocked you out,' Bevis supplied in a low voice as I hesitated.

I looked up at him, relieved that he had seen where this was leading. 'Yes, I'm afraid she did. That vague figure I dreamed about—it was Pamela. I remember now. I heard a sound, and glanced round, and she was there, brandishing something, and then . . . That's all I remember. The next thing I was waking up in hospital, not knowing who I was, and they told me I was Pamela Lane. I had to believe it.'

'So the "pale-coloured" car had nothing to do with it after all,' Bevis said.

'Oh, but it did,' I told him. 'When Pamela left me to die in that fire, she must have driven away in my car. It's a white Capri, Bev. It was *my* car that Alfred Davies saw, and Pamela was driving it. That's what must have happened.'

'I don't understand,' Marjorie said in bewilderment. 'Why should Pamela do such a thing?'

'I can only guess,' I replied. 'When she saw how alike we were . . . When I told her my life

203

was at a crossroads ... I think she planned to swap places with me. We know she had got herself into a mess. If she had killed me, she would have been free of her debts and all her troubles. No one would have thought twice about the identity of a dead body in her cottage. And she could have gone off pretending to be me. My mother is about the only one who would have known the difference, but these days I don't see much of her.'

'Then what was all that about tonight?' Bevis asked. 'Only an hour ago, you ...' He stopped, and sat down on the stone hearth. 'That *was* Pamela, was it?'

'Yes, it was.'

'But ...'

'Please!' I begged him, pressing my fingers to my throbbing temple. 'Let me tell it in sequence or I'll get muddled.'

'You've hurt your head again!' he exclaimed, leaping up and coming to sit beside me. 'Pam ...'

'It's *Susan*! And do stop jumping around, Bev. You're making me dizzy.'

'And *I'm* confused,' Marjorie added. 'Be quiet, Bevis. Let her tell us in her own way.'

'Thank you,' I sighed. 'Now ... we all know what happened after I was taken to hospital. There's no wonder that nothing was familiar to me, or that her wedding ring was so loose on my finger.'

'It was *hers*?' Bevis exclaimed.

'Yes, it was. I'm not married, nor have I ever *been* married. You see, you've put me off my stroke. What was I saying?'

'When you came out of hospital ...' Marjorie prompted.

'Oh—yes. We know about that. But I've found out a little about what Pamela was doing at the same time. I had told her I was going to spend two nights at the Xanadu Motel, and I've discovered that somebody using my name *did* go there for two nights. It must have been Pamela. And then, I think, she must have found out I wasn't dead. Was there something in the newspaper about it?'

'Front page of the local rag,' Bevis told me. ' "Milkman saves widow", or some such thing.'

'So. She knew. And she must have soon found out what was going on—me losing my memory and being brought here.'

'The whole county knew within hours,' Bevis said, 'thanks to the redoubtable Phyllis.'

'Bevis!' Marjorie said sharply, and her son subsided.

'I believe she kept a watch on us,' I continued. 'There's a place in the woods, only a few yards from the cottage, where someone has been sitting for long periods. From there you can see and hear everything that goes on, and you know how often we left that back door open when we were talking.'

'How do you know all this?' Bevis wanted to

know.

'I'm coming to that. On ... Monday, yesterday—was it yesterday? Anyway, when I went back to the cottage, in the afternoon, a car came. A white car. I thought it was you, Bev. When nobody came I went to find out who it was. The boot lid was up. Someone hit me. I suppose she must have bundled me into the boot, but after that I don't know for sure what happened until I found myself nearly drowning in the Doon reservoir. She—it must have been Pamela—had taken off my jeans and shirt and left some of my own clothes by the water, to make it look like suicide.'

'My God!' Bevis was on his feet again, limping about the room.

I looked at Marjorie, who was listening intently, pale with shock. 'A man fished me out and gave me a bed for the night. He didn't ask questions. He was an odd sort of man. I knew I was myself, but since I didn't remember any of the intervening time I assumed it was the evening of the same day I visited Pamela. Then this morning, remembering that I had booked a room at the Motel, I went there ... And that's when I found I'd lost two whole weeks. I didn't feel very well, so I had a sleep and then decided to call on Pamela to see if she could help fill in the gap. I got as far as Butterford before my memory began to function, and when I turned into the lane I suddenly remembered all of it. I stopped, and

206

tried to fathom it out.

'There's a little track leads off the lane. You can put a car in there and hide it from the road. The bushes crowd very close, and there were already scratches on my car, so I wondered if Pamela had hidden it there. Someone's certainly been using it. There's a path been trodden through the undergrowth, leading to the place from where you can see the back of the cottage. And when Pamela herself came out into the yard to feed the cats, with her hair cut just the way mine is, I knew there was no mistake. She'd swapped places back again.'

Bevis hobbled into sight. 'Were you watching when Alan and I went there?'

'Yes, I was. I could hear every word . . . Are you supposed to be using that ankle?'

'Why didn't you show yourself?' he asked.

'To be honest, I didn't feel well enough to face it.'

'Bevis,' Marjorie said suddenly. 'Something will have to be done. I can hardly believe any of this, but if it's true . . .'

'You're right, mother. Will you get Susan a good stiff drink? She looks as though she needs one. I'm going to phone the police.'

*   *   *

We waited at the entrance to Wood End Lane, Bevis and I, in my car. Inspector Anderson had promised to meet us there.

'Are you sure you feel up to this?' Bevis asked.

'I'll manage. I'm just a bit tired and headachy.'

'If I get my hands on her . . .' he muttered.

'You'll keep your temper,' I told him. 'Please, Bev. There's been enough violence.'

After that we waited in silence.

When Inspector Anderson arrived, accompanied this time by a uniformed constable, we told him the gist of the story and he suggested that we should all go to the cottage.

By the light of a police torch, we trod down the gravel path. A light still shone behind the curtains in the kitchen.

Motioning us to stay out of sight, Inspector Anderson knocked on the door.

'Who is it?' came Pamela's voice.

'Police, Mrs. Lane. We'd like to talk to you.'

A few seconds later, he was illuminated by the light from the opening door.

'At this time of night?' Pamela said thickly, snuffling. 'Oh—it's Inspector Anderson, isn't it? What can I do for you?'

'Do you know a Miss Forrester, Susan Forrester?'

'Why, yes. She's my second cousin. Oh—don't tell me. Something's happened to her, hasn't it? She was in such a state when she came to see me. A man had jilted her. She was very depressed. She hasn't . . .'

'She was found in the reservoir at Doon, yesterday evening,' Anderson said, which was the truth, as far as it went.

'Oh my God! I had a feeling it would happen. Poor Sue. But what can I do?'

'Can you tell us when you last saw her?'

'Oh, yes. Yesterday. In the afternoon. I was in the middle of cleaning up when . . . Why don't you come in, Inspector? It's cold, and as you can hear I'm not feeling too well.'

Anderson signalled us to follow and we stepped together into the familiar room, the constable behind us. Pamela stared at me in disbelief, dabbing at her nose with a tissue. Very slowly, she sank down into a chair.

'I thought . . . Inspector, you said . . . what has she been saying?'

'What *is* there to say?' Bevis demanded angrily. He made a movement towards her, but stopped when I touched his arm.

'Where have you been for the past two weeks?' Anderson asked.

'I've been here—and at the Hall. You saw me, only last Saturday.'

'I saw one of you,' Anderson said, looking from one to the other of us. 'Seeing you together, I'm inclined to think it was Miss Forrester I talked to. Look at your hands, and look at hers. The woman I spoke to had just tangled with a rose bush. Where are the scratches, Mrs. Lane?'

She stared at her hands, she stared at me, at the Inspector. 'They've healed.'

He shook his head. 'I don't think so. Mr. Heyman, you're the one who will know. Which of these ladies has been staying at the Hall?'

'Susan has,' Bevis said at once. 'Now that I see you in the light, Pamela, there's no doubt. You miscalculated. Mother and I got to know Susan too well. You would never have fooled us for long. You may look alike, but your personalities are totally different.'

Pamela got to her feet, her face growing old with lines of hatred. 'You! You'll pay for this. I'll stand up in court and tell the world how you wormed your way into my father's affections, in my dead brother's shadow, and how that . . . that woman, acting so sweet and all the time scheming . . . Between you, you robbed me of what was mine by right.'

'All you have to do,' Bevis said quietly, 'is contest the will. It wasn't fair. Any solicitor could have told you that.'

She stared at him blankly. 'But David said . . . David wouldn't let me!'

'But David's dead,' Bevis pointed out, almost gently.

'Get your coat, Mrs. Lane,' Inspector Anderson instructed.

'Can we go?' Bevis asked. 'Susan has had quite enough for one day.'

'Yes, of course. We'll be in touch if we need you. And thank you.'

Hand in hand, we felt our way down the dark path.

'She really was under David's spell, wasn't she?' I said sadly. 'But how could she believe those things she said about you and Marjorie?'

'It's what a lot of people said,' Bevis told me. 'Do *you* believe it?'

'Nobody who really knows you and your mother could believe it.'

Climbing into the Capri, we headed back for the Hall.

'What are you going to do now?' Bevis asked.

'I'll drop you off and then go back to the Motel.'

'Must you?'

'Yes, I think I must, Bev.'

'If you say so.' His voice was sad. 'But ... you'll need to stay around for a while, until all this business is sorted out. You need to rest, or you'll be really ill. There's no point in paying hotel bills, and anyway ... mother's going to need you. Having someone to fuss over will take her mind off what's happening. She's very fond of you, you know. So tomorrow ... come back to the Hall. Will you?'

'I'll see. Talk it over with your mother. Phone me in the morning.'

When I drew up outside the Hall he hesitated, as if he wasn't sure what to do, At last he said, 'I need time to think. Talk to you tomorrow.'

211

'Yes, all right. Goodnight, Bev.'

'Take care of yourself, sweet Sue.' He leaned across suddenly and kissed my cheek before sliding from the car.

*   *   *

The phone woke me just before nine. I struggled awake, grabbing the receiver to stop the awful noise.

'Susan?' Marjorie's voice. 'Oh—did I wake you? I'm sorry, darling, but Bevis has been on at me to phone for the past half hour. I *told* him you'd still be in bed. He says you'll probably listen to me if I tell you . . . You're to come here. I won't listen to any argument. We're expecting you. Goodness me, where else should you stay? . . . Did you hear me?'

'Yes,' I said through sudden tears. 'You're wonderful, Marjorie. I'll be with you in . . . about an hour?'

It was more like an hour and a half before I pulled up outside the front door of Butterford Hall, in pouring rain. Bevis emerged with a brolly and conducted me, carrying my case, into the house, where Marjorie was waiting. She smiled shyly, then rushed to kiss me as if she couldn't contain herself any longer.

'It's *lovely* to have you home!' she exclaimed. 'Oh—excuse me. I mean you must look on this as your home, as long as you're here. Isn't that right, Bevis?'

'Right,' he agreed. 'Mother, take charge of the umbrella, will you? I'll put Sue's case in her room.'

'We've given you another room,' Marjorie confided as she led me into the sitting-room. 'We thought you might prefer it. It's on the front, so you can see over the trees all along the valley. Sit down, now. Phyllis is making coffee.'

'Have you told her about it?' I asked.

'Yes, we have. And I had a word with her about that other business, too. I don't think she really meant any harm.'

When Phyllis brought the coffee, Marjorie invited her to join us, presumably so she didn't feel 'excluded'. We talked over some of the points concerning Pamela and I explained things in a little more detail. Eventually Marjorie and Phyllis went off to the kitchen. 'You two invalids can keep each other company,' Marjorie smiled as she closed the door.

Bevis and I regarded each other uncertainly across the hearth rug. Now that we were alone it was difficult to know what to say.

'That letter you got on Saturday,' he said at length, 'was from your mother, I presume. Pamela must have written to her about your visit to cover her tracks.'

'Yes, it looks that way. She wanted to make it quite clear that she—posing as me—had left the cottage before anything happened.'

213

'And what about that "waking dream" you had at the cottage?'

'I've been wondering about that myself,' I told him. 'If she had been hanging about that day she must have heard what went on, and when she saw you go off for your walk . . .'

'She went into the cottage and acted out a scene for your benefit—to throw suspicion on me.'

'Or simply to make trouble between us. Perhaps we were getting too friendly for her liking, especially as she planned to take up where I left off.'

'Yes,' Bevis said grimly. 'You saw last night how "friendly" she is to me. I don't understand how she ever hoped to carry it off.'

Silence fell between us again. In the hearth, the yellow chrysanthemums that James had brought were beginning to turn brown at the edges.

'I said last night that I had to think,' Bevis said. 'Well, I've thought.'

'Oh? And what conclusions have you reached?'

For answer, he asked a question of his own. 'Who's Paul? Is that who Pamela mentioned—the man who "jilted" you?'

'You could call it that. He preferred someone else. It happens. But I had got over it long before I came to Butterford, I assure you.'

'I love you,' Bevis said abruptly.

I stared at him, my head and heart thudding. 'You don't know me, Bev. It was Pamela you loved.'

'No. It wasn't. That's what I had to think about. I never loved Pamela,. Ten years ago I was young and stupid enough to be flattered by her interest, but that's all it was. Since then I've come to loathe her. It was *you* I fell in love with, whatever name you were called by.'

'And what about Lorraine?'

'Lorraine and I were just friends. As a matter of fact, she realised what was happening before I did. "All you talk about is Pamela, Pamela, Pamela. Are you in love with her or something?"—that's what she said. I denied it, vigorously. But afterwards I realised she was probably right, and I was furious with myself. Susan—I know you don't feel the same way, but I had to explain. I won't embarrass you any further with it, I promise.'

'How do you know I don't feel the same way?' I asked, a catch in my throat.

'It's been painfully obvious.'

'But, Bev, I thought I was your step-sister, didn't I? I thought loving you was hopeless—too many barriers between us. That's why I kept avoiding the subject, not because . . .'

'Sue!' He was out of his chair with a rush, his face alight. I held up my hands to stop him but he came on, pulling me to my feet, into his arms, and when he kissed me I stopped trying to resist. There was no need for resistance now that the barriers had gone.

'You know we're crazy, don't you?' I said against his shoulder. 'We've only known each other two weeks. No, less than that.'

'Some people don't even take that long,' he informed me.

'Yes, but . . .' I looked up at him. 'You don't know the first thing about me, Bev.'

Smiling, he gave me three quick kisses. 'You're a proper little worrier, aren't you? I know all I need to know. But come and sit down. You, my girl, must take it very easy for a while. You're still too pale for my liking. And I had better rest this ankle today. I shall have to get back to work tomorrow . . . There, that's better.' We sat together on the settee, his arm curved round me. 'Comfortable? Right. Now you can tell me your life story. You were born at a very early age, I know. Take it from there. We've got all day.'

We hope you have enjoyed this Large Print book. Other Chivers Press or Thorndike Press Large Print books are available at your library or directly from the publishers.

For more information about current and forthcoming titles, please call or write, without obligation, to:

Chivers Press Limited
Windsor Bridge Road
Bath BA2 3AX
England
Tel. (01225) 335336

OR

Thorndike Press
P.O. Box 159
Thorndike, Maine 04986
USA
Tel. (800) 223-2336

All our Large Print titles are designed for easy reading, and all our books are made to last.